KOLCHAK:
THE NIGHT STALKER

A BLACK & EVIL TRUTH

A NOVEL

BY C.J. HENDERSON

KOLCHAK
CREATED BY JEFF RICE

First MOONSTONE edition 2007

Kolchak: the Night Stalker: A Black and Evil Truth
© 2007 by Moonstone & C.J. Henderson
All Rights Reserved

"Kolchak the Night Stalker" © 2007 by Jeff Rice
All Rights Reserved

ISBN 10 digit: 1-933076-23-2   13 digit: 978-1933076-23-2

Limited Edition Hardcover
ISBN 10 digit: 1-933076-24-0   13 digit: 978-1933076-24-9

Cover painting by Bob Larkin

Art Direction by Dave Ulanski

Book Design and Prepress by Erik Enervold/Simian Brothers Creative

Special thanks to Paul Morris for the assist

Printed in USA

Without limiting the rights of the copyright reserved above, no part of this publication may be reproduced, stored in or introduced into a retrieval system, or transmitted, in any form, or by any means (electronic, mechanical, photocopying, recording, or otherwise), without the prior express written consent of the publisher and copyright holder.

PUBLISHER'S NOTE:
This is a work of fiction. Names, characters, places, and incidents either are the products of the authors' imagination or are used fictitiously, and any resemblance to actual persons, living or dead, business establishments, events, or locales is entirely coincidental.

Published by Moonstone, 582 Torrence Ave, Calumet City, IL 6040
www.moonstonebooks.com

"It is a sin to believe evil of others, but it is seldom a mistake."
-H.L. Mencken

"The belief in a supernatural source of evil is not necessary; men alone are quite capable of every wickedness."
-Joseph Conrad

"To plunder, to slaughter, to steal, these things they misname empire; and where they make a wilderness, they call it peace."
-Tactius

PROLOGUE:

I am going to tell you a story of the greatest evil I have ever known.

As a single, nameable entity it has existed among us unseen and unrecognized since before most people alive today were even born. As an idea, a goal, a desired end, however, it has been with us as long as there were those in the world willing to harm the innocent for their own ends. And that, my friends, is an exceedingly much longer span of time.

Now, I realize that I've been known to have said things like this before. It's true; I've been labeled quite famously in some circles for spreading fear, for shouting "Apocalypse" in a crowded room. My reputation, such as it is anymore, is one of the crank, the hysteric. Some like to label me as an "attention seeker." Well, okay—why not? Throw that one in there, too.

But, before you are distracted by what my detractors think of as the "reasoned debate" of name-calling, ask yourself how often these condemnations have been used to mask what those with their own agendas would have you not see. Think of those "crank" scientists who warned of global warming; remember the hysterics of the small free presses in Poland, Czechoslovakia and a few other places who had their concerns over that Hitler chap. And, was their ever a bigger attention seeker than Cassandra, pointing at that oversized wooden knock-off of Seabisquit, while she muttered something about "Greeks bearing gifts."

We cranks, we're not always wrong, you know.

You can believe as much of what I have to say as you would like. Many will choose to ignore what I am about to tell you, especially considering that little proof remains to back up any of my claims. I can point to the horrific murders and the devastating explosions that rocked the Appalachian Mountains a few months back, as well as to the amazing speed with which so many soldiers were sent in to... now, what were they sent in there to do again, was it? Oh yes, I have the clipping right here:

"To search for survivors, offer assistance to those in need, and to maintain and preserve the public sense of order."

That's right. How could I forget? And while we're on the subject, how could I let it slip my mind that while the Marines were doing all this humanitarian work—the kind they've always been so well known for—that the Red Cross, the Salvation Army and a half dozen other relief agencies from around the world were barred entrance to the disaster area. Hundreds dead, thousands missing, plus the near destruction of a town and a college, one in flames, the other swallowed by the Earth, tens of thousands of acres consumed by fire, bizarre reports of senseless looting and possible multiple homicides during the devastation period... and for some extended period after it as well ...

All of that, and yet no outcry for an investigation. Not by the American public—heavens forbid—not when there was so much else of importance for folks to concern themselves with. Like those photos of top box office action hero Gary Daniels that were suddenly released—was that really his co-star Brenden Campbell feeding him those strawberries, among other things?

And, what with pop diva, Debbie Vish, getting her incredibly messy divorce, and the flurry of marriage proposals showered upon eighty-seven year old Molly Sandlinvic after her winning of the eighteen state wide Boffo-Bucks Sweepstakes—especially with all the fun the media had reporting on the fact that sweet old Molly couldn't even remember buying a ticket. Lucky thing that Quick-Mart cashier remembered her buying one from him. Especially since the silly old dear couldn't remember him, either. Or ever having been in his store. And all those simply charming times she said she'd never gambled in her life. Sigh–old people.

Now, you might ask yourselves, am I suggesting something, dear reader? Could it be that maybe I might be up to my old trick of seeing conspiracies around every corner and dark doings behind every closed door? Perhaps I am, at that. But the only sure way you'll have of knowing is if I go back to the beginning, and tell you the whole, long story. Don't worry, I've done it before; I can do it again.

Of course, this time, going back to the beginning means a slightly longer trip than usual. •

CHAPTER ONE:

On Saturday, April 25, at what has been established as 2:30 A.M., a Ms. Cheryl Ann Hughes was tapping her foot angrily as she waited at the corner of Second and Fremont streets. This was actually a few years back, in a little town all of America knows and loves. The place is called Las Vegas; it's a warm spot—much like at least one other I could mention. And, at 2:30 on the morning in question, Ms. Hughes was only minutes away from becoming the first victim of a cold-blooded fiend, one who would go on to murder a total of five unsuspecting souls—the worst rampage ever known to that charming desert community.

For those not familiar with me, my name is Carl Kolchak, and at that time I was a reporter for the **Las Vegas Daily News**, an establishment about which, the less said the better. I stumbled across the Hughes murder, a rather ordinary incident all in all in Vegas. But as I followed it in the routine manner all those who cover the homicide beat tend to fall into, it lead me along a trail of police mismanagement and cover-up which started me thinking I just might have found my golden story—my long hoped-for meal ticket back to the big leagues.

I had a lot of wonderful theories at first. The killer had to be some-one famous; I was so certain, but then, I had good reason. The way the investigation was being handled simply screamed cover-up. Maybe it was an out-of-control ball player (any type of ball would do), or an entertainer, politician—it didn't matter– whoever had done in poor Cheryl Ann Hughes, it had to be someone with money and influence–enough to make the cops muddy the waters on purpose. I was sure of it.

I was spectacularly wrong.

It turned out the killer was a vampire—yes, you heard me correctly—a vampire, one much like the types so often found in older movies. Not a modern Hollywood vampire— all fangs and wings, bent and hairy— but one who looked mostly human, who dressed nicely, who lived alone except for the women he kept tied to a bed to supply him with late-night snacks.

As the facts I gathered fell into place, it became clear the police were indeed covering something up, but it was nothing more than the usual— their gross incompetence, as well as their inability to comprehend anything not covered in their manuals. Rigidly, they refused to admit what the facts right before their faces screamed at them—that they were indeed chasing a monster, but one not escaped from an insane asylum, but from the pages of legend.

Ultimately, as the only person in all of Las Vegas who would take the truth those facts spelled out seriously, it was left to me to dispatch this creature. Now please, do not labor under any delusions, dear reader, that I did so in the guise of a white knight or any other sort of noble avenger. I did so with a palpable terror in my heart, and the only reason I did so at all was because I was half-blackmailed into doing it. The other half of the push that was strong enough to get me to pit myself against such a creature was built on lies, many of them told to me by my own greed, which flattered me to the point where I forgot what a good friend my common sense had always been to me.

As I was thrown out of Las Vegas after rendering it a service beyond any sane person's imaginings, I vowed I would never turn my back on this good friend ever again. To this day, I do not believe I have done so, at least, not consciously. I may have doubted its advice for a moment or two, weighing it to make certain it wasn't running away with me, this much is certainly possible. But doubt it? No—not on your life.

Never again.

And for good reason. After being pitched headlong into oblivion by the fine folks of the Las Vegas Tourism Board, I found my fortunes much reduced—which was quite a tragedy considering the point from where such reductions started. I had thought the **Vegas News** was as far down the journalistic food chain as my descent from my "glory days" in New York and Chicago could possibly take me. I was, in a word, wrong—colossally wrong. Spectacularly wrong. Indeed, before much time could pass, I found myself grateful for by-lines appearing in rags that made **the National Inquirer** look like the **New York Times**.

Something I did find amazing at the time, however, was that as

I wandered across the country from city to city, looking for each new lower berth that might find my brand of copy editorially pleasing, was that in each new town I determined to make my home, I was preceded by a familiar face. Tony Vincenzo is a small, dried-out Brooklyn-born Sicilian. And yes, while it is certainly true that the wonderful borough of Brooklyn is the home of many a famous son, when thinking of Vincenzo, only the Three Stooges come to mind. He has been a newsman, and I use the term loosely, since those ancient days in which the front page was still set with hot lead, and yet I swear he himself does not possess ambition or curiosity enough to look outside to see if it's raining.

Do not let my exasperated tone lead you to think of him as a lazy or untalented individual. Managing editors of great metropolitan papers, and the other kind, might not need be imbued with much creativity, but they must possess a strong work ethic, and Vincenzo fits that bill enough for three men. He is hardworking to the point of ulcers, and clever enough in his own right to have brought praise to the doorsteps of some very unnoteworthy rags.

What he is not, however, is daring. Vincenzo is not one to take a leap—ever. In fact, so frightened of the concept is he, the man will walk around a hopscotch game chalked on the sidewalk, rather than risk being drawn into somehow skipping a step. He is a turtle of an editor, retreating into his shell at the least sign of a scoop.

Am I unfair? Perhaps. But as anyone over the age of twelve can tell you, it's not really me that's unfair. It's life that maintains that condition. I merely report on it.

The point I am wandering away from here is that for some reason I had foolishly marked it down to simply "Fate," no matter where I went looking for work, after a city of two, there would be Vincenzo, willing to hire me once more.

To give him his due credit, he was not fired from the **Las Vegas Daily News**; he quit over what they had done to me. He did not seek me out afterward—that would have been a little too much of a show of sentimentality for him. But when I stumbled across him, he did start handing me checks in exchange for words once again, which was his way of apologizing, I suppose. Needing to eat, I declined to refuse them. I'm marvelously gracious that way.

Things might have been fine for us as the Abbott and Costello of the print media (he is the short, round one, for those keeping score), except for one minor flaw I failed to keep under control. For some reason, after my run-in with a real life, actual out-of-the-grave, neck-chewing vampire, I suddenly could not turn the corner without running into something else from the Universal Studios hall of classics.

Before I knew it, and please believe me, much against my will, I found myself face to face with a werewolf. And a witch. And zombies, bargain basement Jack the Rippers, aliens, golems and swamp creatures. Try as I might to simply cover lying government officials, mass murderers or even dog shows and the garden beat, every so often, without trying, without looking for them, demons and ghosts and mummies—even *mummies*, for God's sake—kept throwing themselves in my path.

I would, of course, continue to report on them. I would, of course, be thwarted at every turn by my reliable Brooklyn-born tortoise. And eventually, we would both find ourselves in another city, struggling to reinvent ourselves once more. That would work for a while, the Twilight Zone would leave me alone for a bit, and then suddenly some devil would start pulling people into mirrors or a suit of armor would start committing murders, and I'd be forced to start the whole terrible process rolling again.

But, you ask, couldn't I have simply turned my back on such stories? And the answer is, well yes, certainly, given that the concept of free will is an actual and real thing, I could have. But, when I think of how "sensible" it might have been to do so, I think of those who called the scientists warning the world of global warming "cranks." And I think back on the hysterics of the small free presses in Poland and Czechoslovakia and everywhere else in Eastern Europe that held death camps and gas chambers where people were herded like cattle and murdered by the train car load. I think of the hundreds of thousands, the *millions,* who were slaughtered by bullets and gas and fire, their mouths searched for gold teeth, their body fat rendered down to make soap, their skin stripped from their shrunken frames to make lamp shades—all because not one single newsman had the guts to stop being "sensible" and tell the world.

I think on that and the Cassandra in me boils to the surface again whether I like it or not. This is not said to make those offering reasonable council feel stupid or low or cowardly. It is merely offered to explain why one might submit themselves to constant ridicule and humiliation. A newsman's job is to look for news and to report it.

Please understand, I don't hunt monsters. I'm not a crusader, an avenger, or some other character you might find on your television, but never in real life. It's not my sworn job to stop evil. It's my sworn job to report on the activities of evil—to keep a light focused on it so that its hopefully loathsome decay will not spread like rust on wheat.

And so, I have tried my best to do this. My results have been mixed at best. Sometimes I report that fact and feel proud that I have done so well. At other times I look at the same record of achievement and wonder how I could have accomplished so little. It's all a matter of perspective, I imagine. Or how much I've had to drink.

And, now that I have told you what lead me to my current dilemma, you should have enough information to judge my record for yourselves. If, after I tell you the monstrous truth I uncovered in the mountains of Virginia, you find yourselves thinking I did all I could, I will accept such judgment as graciously as I know how. If, however, your verdict is that I have been a puppet and a fool who has caused more trouble and pain than I could ever compensate for with my minor victories, I confess I am ready to accept that conclusion just as readily.

In other words, I turn to you because I have lost all feeling in that part of my soul which can tell right from wrong. The scope of damnation has drifted beyond my perception. In the desperate hope that it is not beyond yours, I begin my tale at last. ●

CHAPTER TWO

It was a Sunday, the first after Thanksgiving, at roughly 3:00 A.M. that the first of the murders in question took place. The victim to be was Wendel Halford, the night shift foreman at the Happy Holland Frozen Yogurt plant outside of the undistinguished hamlet of Two Hollows, West Virginia. Stepping outside for a much needed cigarette break, he had no way of suspecting that not only was he about to die, but that he would do so in a manner which would terrify the nation.

Halford was a big man, a outdoorsman with twenty-two years experience in the wilderness. Granted, this was the modern, hemmed in wilderness where deer and rabbits were just as likely to be brought down by soccer moms in their SUVs as they were the skilled eye of a crafty hunter, but it was experience nonetheless. Enough so that he should not have died as he did.

Wendel Halford was acknowledged to possess an extremely cool head, and an even keener eye. He knew and understood the sounds and ways of the forest—could track across rock and water, and could tell when and where things were moving in the brush even when visibility was impossible. At least, that was the opinion of his friends and family in and around Two Hollows.

That Sunday night, however, some deficiency in Halford's expertise manifested itself. For some reason none could determine, the skilled eye did not see whatever it was that approached him. His seasoned ears heard nothing which might have preserved him. In short, his many and varied woodsman's abilities in no way betrayed the fact that while he stood in the semi-circle of light shining down from above the back door of the loading dock, that for the first time in his life, he had become the hunted.

Something came out of the forest surrounding the Happy

Holland plant, something that wished to stalk Wendel Halford. Something quiet enough to scale a cyclone fence without making noise enough to be heard. Something clever enough to approach a seasoned hunter without being noticed. And, something large enough, and strong enough, possessed of claws and fangs and teeth sharp enough, something the innermost soul of which was vicious enough to tear poor Wendel Halford into quite a number of broken, bloodied pieces.

The local crime scene investigation team had little trouble identifying the victim for, as messy and terrible as the murder of the nightshift foreman was, he proved remarkably easy to reassemble. Though savagely ripped apart, all the pieces of Halford were still present there on the grounds. Nothing of the man had been removed. Indeed, no part whatsoever of Halford had proved tantalizing enough for whatever had sunk its teeth into him to do any chewing or swallowing.

And this is the one small fact which set the nation to quivering. After all, even in a society as easily, readily and constantly distracted as ours, it's one thing for a man to be attacked by a bear or a puma or something else that made a habit of indiscriminately separating other creature's flesh from its bones. It was another, however, that once all such separations had been made, that the separator would then simply discarded all those carefully carved bits and pieces.

"It was all there, and I'll tell you the truth," Jedediah Peterson, the local Two Hollows coroner was quoted as saying by one of our country's less tasteful weekly print rags. "I swear if we bothered to try and reclaim all of Halford's blood, we'd find every drop of that, too."

I suppose it had been a slow news week, for across the country in my own Los Angeles, in the North Hollywood offices of my beloved **Hollywood Dispatch**, the two-hundred-and-fifty-eight pound boiled tomato known as Tony Vincenzo and I found ourselves deep in debate over what might possibly be behind the slaughter of poor, torn-apart nicotine fiend, Wendel Halford.

"Com'on, Carl, give—" Vincenzo needled at me. "You of all people must have some crazy theory about this. Man torn apart by wild beast. The type of tracks recovered prove to be of unknown origin. Saliva untraceable to known species. Silent killer rips man apart but doesn't even lick up a mouthful of blood. Aren't you tingling to get out your Junior Men In Black kit and start analyzing this one?"

I stared as if Vincenzo had grown another head to join the two he already had.

"Or have you got it all figured out already? Tell me, Carl, is it the last voyage of the Hanover all over again?"

"Excuse me," I answered. "Is this really my sober unto boredom editor-in-chief suggesting that our poor nation, which surely has troubles enough just keeping the current administration from putting the Constitution in a shredder, has been blessed with another werewolf?"

"Speculate with me, Carl. Give that sixth grade imagination of yours some freedom."

"I can't take this seriously," I told him, my eyes spinning in wild circles of their own volition. "After how many years of quashing, stalling, burying and outright murdering stories out from under me—stories, I will remind you with the ferocity of a mother lion guarding her cubs, I'd thoroughly researched—you now want to indulge your whimsy factor on fanciful werewolves?"

Vincenzo spread his hands out in front of him, using the motion to push his shoulders upward enough to complete a shrug. He was bored. We had put the front page to bed, and pretty much had the next week outlined. Ad revenues were up. And, best of all, someone must have been passing out stupid pills on Rodeo Drive for days because the amount of entertainment notables making headline-worthy morons out of themselves had suddenly made working at **the Hollywood Dispatch** one of the easiest jobs in the world. It still wasn't rewarding, but at least it was getting easier.

Except, of course, when the editor-in-chief decided on a lark that he wanted to amuse himself. Frankly, it boiled me to have him suddenly seeming to take my supernatural run-ins seriously simply because he was too lazy to pull out whatever lurid paperback he had hidden in his bottom drawer and do a little reading. Annoyed, I answered:

"All right, let's say this is some kind of creature from beyond, what's its motivation?"

"What? What are you talking about?"

"You want to play, Tony, I can play. But all games have rules. Okay, this is a werewolf. Sure, why not? But, was there a full moon that night?" While Vincenzo dithered for a moment, I moved around to his side of the desk and stabbed at his keyboard until I called up the weather website the paper uses. Skimming back over the phases of the moon, I pointed out triumphantly to him:

"There, see?" I told him, returning to my chair. "Days away from the full moon. No werewolf."

"Okay, so it's not a werewolf. So what is it, Carl?"

"How would I know? Have I seen the reports, the remains, been on site? Questioned anyone there? It could have been anything. Maybe it was a bear."

"Too heavy," countered Vincenzo. "A bear big enough to kill Halford couldn't have gotten over the cyclone fence without leaving traces. No tracks of any kind found, either."

"I don't know," I answered, willing to play, but not really taking the game all that seriously. "Maybe it pole-vaulted over. Yogi could get pretty creative, you know. Was there a picnic basket on the loading dock?"

"Get serious, Kolchak. We're talking about a man's life here." Vincenzo took a swallow from his coffee cup, then pointed at me, asking, "you're always running into aliens. Maybe it was spacemen. You know, like those cattle mutilations we used to hear about all the time."

"My God," I said, sitting up a bit straighter, "you've done it. You've finally gone insane."

"What are you telling me, Carl? You lost your edge? No more ink left in the veins? Or maybe you're just bucking for some lesser post, something like Emily Cowles used to handle for us back at INS— you know, society news, advice to the lovelorn... something for this new, less motivated you."

"You...," I had some creative phrasing prepared, but I choked it off. A warning buzzer had gone off in the back of my head, alerting me to the fact that the turtle was up to something. Pulling the growl out of my voice, I basically capitulated to what my instincts told me was a safer position. Going in calmer, I tried:

"All right, no bears. Fine, maybe it was wolves then. Wolves chew people up from time to time."

"What about the fence?"

"So they dug under it."

"No holes found. That's what so tantalizing about this case, Carl. It's a locked room murder mystery. The Sunday after Thanksgiving, the plant wasn't running. Halford was there doing machine inspections, one of only four people on the entire site. The police have ruled out the other three. So who, or what, killed Wendel Halford?"

For whatever reason, Vincenzo, irritating little slug that he was, had me intrigued. I had skimmed a few articles on the case. Halford's co-workers had been cleared, not only because their manner alone had proclaimed they were nothing more than horrified bystanders, but by the fact that none of them had even a molecule of Halford's blood on them, nor had a spec of it been found anywhere inside of the Happy Holland facility.

There were vulgar splashes of it all over the loading dock, even up and down the very door Halford had used to reach his beloved out-of-doors for the last time. But nothing inside. No one had slaughtered him and then gone inside the yogurt plant to clean up. In fact, no one had cleaned up at all. Blood had followed the tracks leading back out of Happy Holland. Scarlet gore had been found all about the exit tracks, and up the cyclone fence, even on the other side.

As I ruminated on the question, I caught a look in Vincenzo's eyes which I did not like. It was the self-satisfied glow of a cat, one that could barely contain its glee as it watched an unsuspecting rodent from behind. My eyes narrowing with justifiable suspicion, I asked:

"What?"

"Oh, nothing, Carl. Nothing at all. I'm just simply glad to see you so willing to think hard on this case. And, I'm especially glad to see that 'hell thing' isn't your first guess at what did in the Happy Hooter's foreman …"

"Holland," I corrected.

"What?"

"Holland, Happy Holland Frozen Yogurt. That's the name of the plant."

"See that, you've got the facts straight already. That's what we like about you, Carl. You're such a professional."

"Vincenzo …"

"That's why we're sending you to Virginia to look into this for the **Dispatch**."

"You have to be kidding," I sputtered. "This is old news. It's stale. It's not about some model getting her chest inflated or her lips done over. There's no interest, at least not for our discerning readers. Why would we bother?"

"Because," answered Brooklyn's answer to Stalin, a smile that could have frightened nations spreading across his face, "it just came over the wire an hour ago—the town of Gore, Virginia, less than twenty miles from sleepy, quaint little Two Hollows, West Virginia, just registered its own murder."

As I reeled from the news, Vincenzo's smile widened as he threw a handful of facts at me.

"Yes, it seems Yogi's gone on a bit of a rampage. Another body discovered, torn to shreds. No theft, no sexual abuse, no motive anyone can see. No clues. Just another completely solid blank wall. Your favorite kind of case, isn't it, Carl?"

I stood next to his desk too flabbergasted to reply. Finding that just delightful, Vincenzo chuckled as he added:

"Mr. Ranger's not going to like this, is he?" ●

CHAPTER THREE

"You can't do this to me, Vincenzo."

"Already done, Kolchak."

"Tony ..."

"See Irene on your way out. She's got your voucher slips and your plane tickets."

"You, you have tickets already?" I found myself somewhat startled at my usually reliable tortoise's new-found speed. Such unspecies-like behavior can be disturbing when displayed by a critter with which you believe yourself quite familiar. Trying to bring rationality back to my world, I asked: "I thought you said this just came in in the last few hours?"

"It did; came across Slate's desk this morning." Suddenly I had a cynical glimmer as to where all the excess energy had been found. *Dispatch* publisher Morgan Slate is not what you would call my greatest supporter in the journalism racket. He doesn't so much doubt my talents, as he does dislike my face.

"He called me into his office as soon as he saw it."

Chuckling, Vincenzo slid his feet up onto his desk at that moment, stretching back to emphasize his enjoyment of the situation. His beefy arms linked behind his head, no sanitation union boss ever looked more smug.

"And...?" I asked, fishing for the answer that would hang my darling editor.

"And," he told me with a wheezing glee, "it was decided, immediately I might add, that we should send someone out there." His eyes taking on that demonic gleam I've grown to recognize, he added, "Oh, and don't start feeling abused and start trying to work up your patented brand of righteous indignation. You've got nothing to stand on this time."

You know the place I was in at that moment. Everyone has been there. It's that spot where you stand glued, knowing the galling bastard who has put you there is not bluffing, but needing to see his cards, anyway. Figuring it was a penny-ante game that I'd already lost, I demanded:

"And why not?"

"Because, Kolchak, all the **Dispatch** staff members who know how to be here on time declined the assignment. Guess how many that left?"

I stewed inside, but he was painfully correct; I had nowhere to go. I sputtered for a few seconds, searching for an exit, grasping for something at least witty to throw back, but the sound only gave Vincenzo more satisfaction. Chuckling, he stretched his basketball of a body out further, adding:

"I'll tell you how many that left—that left you. Your tickets were purchased and printed out about a half hour ago."

"But, Tony...," I whined, "have a heart ..."

"Have a nice trip."

"Tony, old friend, old pal ..."

"Can the banana oil, Kolchak. You don't have the time to waste. You, 'old friend, old pal,' you had better start gathering some bags so you can do your packing. Maybe the local grocery store can help you out. Because you've got a flight to catch in less than four hours ..."

"Now I mean it," I huffed, worried I was really up against it. "You can't do this to me, Vincenzo. It's cold in Virginia this time of year. I mean honest, **real** cold. I can't go there—I don't even think I own an overcoat anymore."

I was in full whine by that point. I know it; I admit it. As bad as some of our problems here are, one does get used to the year long joy which is the golden weather of Los Angeles. Now, I will admit that I never thought it would happen to me. My years in New York and Chicago had been during some of the most brutal winters those wonderful cities have ever known. Citizens of both towns wear their survival of such seasons as badges of honor, thinking on them fondly, the way they do making it through transit strikes, or gang wars.

Trust me, I'm no different. Looking at the prospect of wandering about the countryside through the frozen mountains of Virginia with winter approaching no longer looked like a challenge to me. It looked like hell. Hitting middle age takes the fun out of freezing one's ass off for most people. Still, that part of my mind that keeps me from making a complete idiot out of myself from time to time began throwing comments out to me at that moment.

This was no ordinary story, it reminded me. This was a homicide—and, as of just a short while ago, most likely a serial homicide. And, the back of my mind threw in, a sensational homicide. This was a story about a maniac who tore people into little bitty meatballs for no apparent reason. The kind of stuff no one wrote better than I do.

I could, of course, the voice reminded me, continue to feel put upon. It assured me I had that right. But, it also reminded me that the **Hollywood_Dispatch** does not employ all that many real reporters. Walking bundles of soggy cheesecloth like Ron Updyke, sadly, probably my main competitor for by-lines these days, were not newsmen. No, my "peers" at the **Dispatch**, a horrible reminder of just how low I had sunk, were not newsmen at all. They were the kind of hacks who stuffed press kits into their blenders and then reassembled the shards into the drivel upon which they slapped their names.

Vincenzo and I might have the antagonistic relationship of a cobra and a mongoose, but we had their level of respect for each other as well. Tony wasn't sending me to Virginia to punish me; he was doing it because he had no choice. If Slate wanted the story covered—and a maniac who tore people apart for no apparent reason was definitely our kind of story—even he had to admit it was a waste of money to send anyone from our festering boil of a publication other than myself.

"You're looking all thoughtful, Carl," my darling tortoise said with a shade of worry. "Things are turning over in that mushbowl you call a skull, aren't they?"

"Somewhat," I admitted. "Partially. I get a rent-a-car, correct?"

"Yes, Carl... you get a motel room, too."

"*Motel?* Surely you're just experiencing a bit of consonant trouble. You meant to use an 'H' there, as in 'hotel,' preferably one with four or more stars somewhere in its title."

"There's a number in its title somewhere," Vincenzo growled, "and it's at least one digit higher than five, but that's all there is to that."

"I'll be taking the new digital camera with me," I said, getting into the spirit of things, "and a company cell phone." The turtle's head came most of the way out of its shell at that one. Before he could start snapping his amphibian maw, however, I cut him off, saying:

"Now, Tony—you want me staying in touch, don't you? Getting expenses approved, not making a step without your express permission ..."

"This is *Carl* Kolchak I'm speaking to, isn't it?"

"Oh," I answered, my mouth dropping to a non-butter-melting temperature, "and I'll need that new laptop Updyke keeps taking home with him."

"Hey, now wait a minute—that thing's expensive ..."

"Then let's finally put it to some use that might justify having bought it," I answered. "All Updyke uses it for is writing chapters of his idiot sci fi novel."

"Really ...?"

I almost felt sorry for my little turtle over that one. I couldn't believe it, but I guess he believed my "peer" when he told our shared editor that he needed the laptop nearly every night of the week to brush up his articles about stolen bicycles and lost puppies. Grabbing a handful of extra pens and a couple of spiral pads from Tony's side drawer, I added:

"Oh, yes—'The Rocketmen of Yesterday's Tomorrow.' Check a document entitled 'Updyke—personal.' The star is a brave cadet, Roger Upton. You'll like his commanding officer, too, a low comedy kind of buffoon named Toby Vincento."

Seeing the rate of steam flowing from Vincenzo's ears I was hoping for, I headed for the door, throwing over my shoulder:

"It's really quite entertaining."

I held my laughter in as I heard the intercom on Updyke's desk roar to life. I would have stayed to watch the ensuing fun, but I've seen such things before. And besides, I had a plane to catch and a couple of juicy murders to look into.

I've had worse days, I reminded myself as I headed for the door. Little did I know that I would be giving all the worst days of my life an all-out run for their money in just forty-eight short hours. ●

CHAPTER FOUR

My seemingly endless string of plane rides were at least things without any major incidents. I'm not a big enthusiast for heavier than air travel, nor am I a member of the Legion of the Frightened that needs to head for the bar an hour before a flight to get up their nerve. Not that I've ever minded a trip to the bar, but that has nothing to do with airplanes. No, I'm one of those people who wishes there was something faster, something more comfortable and less irritating, but until it comes along I'm happy enough to put up with jets.

What I am not happy these days about is having to put up with the ridiculous levels of security we now have everywhere. Because of the out of the way nature of my eventual destination, I had to take three flights, each on a successively smaller aircraft. It's bad enough that because of one looney tune we all now have to take our shoes off in major airports. No big deal, you scoff. Try it knowing you have the toe out of one sock and the heel out of the other. Scoff some more, but its the best pair I own.

What was truly ridiculous was having to do so again at the Atlanta hub before I boarded a tiny thirty-seater for the second leg of my journey to Richmond. Who exactly did they think was going to want to blow up a rickety, second-class commuter jet, especially the day when the most important person on the thing was myself? Yes, we were within a few hundred miles of Washington, D.C., but you can't do a whole lot of damage with a plane that weighs less than a school bus.

Still, they didn't bother me on the six-seater I took from Richmond up to the quaint shire of Leesburg, so I won't bother going into any more of it here. You either already agree with me about the lunatic proportions to which our airport security is mismanaged, or you don't. That's not the subject at hand.

No, what I was there for was the investigation of what was beginning to look like the big story for the holiday season. Sitting in what was essentially a converted cropduster on my flight into Leesburg, the notion hit me that if I could get a shot of whatever this killer was coming down a chimney, I could do for Christmas Eve what "Psycho" did for taking showers. Yes, I admit it was a morbid notion, but I had little else to occupy my mind at that moment.

All I knew about either murder was what I had gleaned from the papers. I'd picked up every rag I could at all my various airports du jour, and there was little variation to be found no matter the state I was in or the size of the paper. That meant, of course, that not too much major interest had been thrown toward this case—yet. I had a definite feeling that Slate may have made a wise guess on this one.

Something was definitely up in the countryside between Gore and Two Hollows. There was just not the slightest possibility of uncovering what it was by reading the out-of-town papers. All they gave, when you skinned away the sensationalism and the speculation, was that there had been two ruthlessly horrible murders, most likely committed by the same perpetrator, or a remarkably insightful copy-cat.

That was it.

So far, they had no fingerprints, no forensic evidence of any kind, at least none they were willing to talk about. Human, animal, vegetable, no one would comment on what they thought was shredding people like iceberg lettuce for a neighborhood rib joint's salad bar. It was a tantalizing case, on the surface, and I was hoping my eventual reaching of Gore was not going to lead to any kind of spectacular disappointment.

My arrival in Leesburg offered no indication I would meet with such a fate. I talked for an extended period with both the bartender there at the airport, and with the slightly plump, cutely freckled high school graduate at the rent-a-car stand. Neither of them had the ready kind of answer I was dreading.

I'm certain you've experienced something similar in your lives. You hear about something down the road that sounds exotic and fascinating. But, the closer you get to it, suddenly, the more ordinary it becomes. The back of my mind had been cautioning me since Vincenzo's office that, what sounded wild and monstrous to those sitting behind desks in big cities, could turn out to be just an ordinary act of nature once I got to the sticks.

But, no—it seemed I was in luck. Fred, my bartender, he perked up when I asked him his opinion on the murders as if it was the first conversation he'd been offered in a year and a half. He didn't have any extra information, but he was a hunter, and during the winter season, a trapper, and he'd never heard of anything like it, not even, as he put it, "in the old stories." Fred turned out to be part Native American, mustn't say "Indian" these days, you know, which explained the trapping, as well as his knowledge of local legends.

"No, sir, Mr. Kolchak," he told me and my tape recorder, and by extension, all the readers of the **Dispatch**, "it's not a natural thing at all. You go back through the tales that have been handed down in this area for the last thousand years, you won't find anything like this. This thing, whatever it is ... this is something new."

I told Fred he would be known as "Native American shaman Fred Warmspirits, keeper of the healing waters." He thought that was amusing enough to offer to buy me a drink. Not to offend him, I allowed him to do so.

Debbie, as her name-tag christened her, or Deborah Sue Warner, as she was simply busting to tell you, was not nearly as diverse a find as Fred (whose actual tribal name I didn't even wonder about until I met the fiercely proud Ms. Warner). She was, however, young, and impressionable. She was a fan of horror movies, in that she liked to go to them and scream, and she was more than willing to discuss everything she had heard about the murders.

I could report on our conversation at length, but all it boiled down to was the simple fact that people in and around the area had been buzzing since the first murder, and now that there was a second, well, if Martians landed tomorrow, it would be but a minor distraction to them.

Yes, people were killed every now and then in Northwestern Virginia, as well as right next door in Eastern West Virginia. Stores were robbed, house burglaries went wrong there as well. Drug deals could go just as sour in the Appalachians as they could on the streets of Detroit—just not with nearly the regularity. But killings done with guns and knives and clubs were so much more easily understood. As Ms. Warner told me:

"Oh, it's got people jumpy, that's a fact. And we're way over here in Leesburg. It don't matter, though. Not hardly. It's got folks craning their necks at every little noise, let me tell you. My parents haven't ever locked their doors before; maybe when they went on vacation, or down to Richmond for a day of shopping, something like that, but now—now they're keeping them locked all the time. And I don't blame them."

When I got into my rental, a non-descript hatchback painted the ugliest shade of green ever invented, I could not have been happier. Ms. Warner was the target audience of the **Hollywood Dispatch**, young, under-educated, frivolous and a touch pretentious. Those easily caught up in lurid nonsense will keep slapping their money down for something that seems like a real newspaper but reads like tabloid television. If she was giddy over these murders, willing to speculate on end with a complete stranger about what it could all be about, it was a guarantee this thing had the legs of a thoroughbred.

I was as happy as a half-frozen man could be.

The hatchback had a decent enough heater that I did not put my limited expense money at risk buying an overcoat at an airport clothing outlet. I had decided that since such a thing would have to be considered a luxury item in LA, I would wait until I got close to the scene, and then look for a second hand store where I could pick one up for pocket change.

Virginia Primary Road 7 took me to the large enough town of Winchester where it was clear I could have found an adequate-enough piece of apparel, if only anything were still open. I had spent most of the day waiting for planes, and the rest of the day in them. Not wanting to risk my motel room being cancelled on me, I drove straight through to Gore, transferring to Primary 50 on the other side of Winchester, and then to Secondary 751 for the last few miles into town.

And, actually I didn't have to go all the way into town. My lodgings turned out to be in a place called "Motel 1,2,3!" for some reason not readily evident. It was hidden away on the outskirts of Gore, which was fine enough for me. The day was gone, and I was tired. Being noble, I asked the desk clerk how far it was to the crime scene.

"You a reporter, ain't you?" When I assured him I was, he grinned with apparent self-satisfaction, explaining:

"I knew it. I mean, I didn't know you was a reporter, but I knew you guys would be showin' up."

"Because of the murders ..."

"Yes, sir; that's right. This is too big, you know? Too weird, you know? Just way too darn big. Bet there's gonna be a whole lot more of you before too long, too. You know?"

I assured him I had an inkling of what he was talking about, which is why, I reminded him, I had asked him how far it was to the crime scene. Nodding, he said:

"Oh, it ain't far, but you ain't gonna get in. Not now. It's too late."

The second murder had been committed behind a strip mall, according to the papers. A non-resident, modern society's polite euphemism for what we used to simply call a hobo, had met his end behind a tiny conglomerate of local businesses and two fast food outlets. Going through the trash, he had been brutally transformed into a part of it, then left there to be found in the morning.

The last of the mall's late-nighters had closed down for the evening two hours before I arrived. That, I thought, might not pose that great a problem since what I wanted to view was the outside of the premises, and the backside of them at that. Still, my eager clerk informed me:

"Yeah, I get what you mean, you know? But the sheriff, Sheriff Jeeter, he put the word out that no one would be 'llowed near the... ah, lemme get that paper ..."

The clerk fumbled through some sheets on his desk, then pulled free a sheet of old-style fax paper. I caught sight of a police-style logo on the top of the page. The clerk read:

"'No one will be granted access to the crime scene without a proper escort. No one will be granted an escort except during the hours from 10 A.M. to 4 P.M. Any seeking access without an escort will be liable to prosecution, punishable by a fine, imprisonment, or both.'"

I was informed that Jeeter had made certain these notifications made it to every place of lodging, gas station, convenience store and the such anywhere in or around the entire town, as well as for twenty or thirty miles up each road outside of Gore as well. The sheriff was obviously not a stupid man, and like Morgan Slate could foresee the potential in this story. Thinking like a typical lawman, it looked as if he was going to keep as tight a lid on things as he could from the beginning.

My clerk, who finally revealed himself to be a "Roy," asked if I wanted him to read more. I told him he had done a fine job of getting across the gist of things. I also told him I was tired and could probably learn as much at 10 A.M. in the sunlight as I could past midnight in the dark. Extremely content to take my key and to head for a hot shower and bed, I thanked Roy for his help and turned back toward the door. Before I could get outside, however, one last clerking duty forced Roy to call out.

Catching my attention, he let me know he had almost forgotten to give me a letter that had come for me. That, of course, made me curious, because it shouldn't have been possible for anyone to mail me something at that address and have it get there before I did. Roy let me know it was hand- delivered. That fact did not kill my curiosity, but it did offer at least a few possibilities. I looked the envelope over for a moment, checking it for clues as to how right or wrong my private guesses might be.

It was a white, letter-sized envelope, one with a light blue watermark that kept it from being read by anyone holding it up to the light. It had no return address, no stamp, nothing on the outside of it at all except the words "Carl Kolchak."

Seeing no further reason to wait, I shoved a fingernail under the well-glued down flap and struggled for a moment until I could get a finger inside. Then I tore the thing open and pulled forth the letter within. As prepared as I thought I was for anything, the ten words inside caught me complete off-guard.

Then, as I read them a second, then a third time, they filled me with a dread so utterly complete it took all I could do to keep from shaking. ●

CHAPTER FIVE

"Did you see who delivered this?"

"No, sorry," apologized Roy. "I went in the back for a few minutes earlier today... to make use of the facilities, you know. When I came back, there it was on the counter. At first I didn't know what it was, but then, I mean, your name is kinda the kind you remember, you know?"

"Yeah," I told him off-handedly, my eyes scanning the parking lot.

"What I mean is, I remembered seein' your name on the reservations list. So, I just put it up in the box with your key. Figured you'd know what it is." Roy took a moment to actually come back to the real world and notice that I was no longer the carefree, happy traveler that had first entered his warm but rough sanctuary. His eyes following mine out into the parking lot, he asked in a whisper:

"Did I do something wrong, or something? I mean, is everything, like okay?"

Not needing the noble, helpful Roy to become the panicked, useless Roy, a creature who could only do me ill by talking about my own panic, I turned to him as if I had completely lost track of everything, then asked him:

"Excuse me, what did you say?"

"I asked if I did something wrong—if everything is okay? I mean, like are you all right?"

"Oh—oh I'm sorry," I gushed, turning on all the false charm I could muster. Shoving the letter into my bag, I laughed, shaking my head at the same time, searching for a tone that would tell Roy I was just a senile old reporter momentarily lost in thought. Finding a tone I thought might get that across, I lied:

"I must be getting old. Everything okay? Oh, sure, sure. You remember how you said this thing, the murders, how it was going to pull in more reporters ...?"

"Ah, yeah...?"

"Well, one of my pals must be here, knew I was coming in, and decided he was going to play a joke on me. Please accept my apologies. I'm sorry, but I just started wondering who it might be, and then, before I knew it, I was lost inside my own head wondering. Gettin' old, I guess."

"Oh, okay then."

Roy looked visibly relieved. I had a feeling he was the kind of employee who made mistakes from time to time, and who couldn't afford to lose the job he had. Pulling out a ten, I thanked him for making certain I got the note. Then, acting as if it were an afterthought, I asked him to keep an eye out for anyone trying to leave me another one. My performance extended to mugging broadly over how sweet it would be if he could help me out-maneuver anything further my "pal" might have in store for me. I also let him know if said "pal" could be made to look foolish there would be at least a twenty in it for him—thus, I hoped, defusing him from thinking about the situation overly.

After that, I purposely downplayed the incident further by telling him about my outerwear predicament, and asking his advice on a good place in town where I could pick up something warm to wear. I also let him know that since I would be going back to LA, and most likely leaving it behind, that I wasn't looking to spend much on it. He assured me he would think on the problem. I thanked him for his assurance.

After that, I turned down his suggestion that he make me something for dinner, an offer which would have meant his firing up his own private kitchen—a hotplate in the back of his office. Feigning a need for some rest, pretending that the ten words I had shoved out of sight hadn't driven all fatigue from my body, replacing it with a restless nervousness I knew was going to keep me awake for hours, I gave out with my best phony yawn and headed for room 717.

Once there I threw my bags on the bed, locked the door behind me, made certain the drapes were completely closed, then I sat down on the bed and got the letter out once more. Unfolding it gently, as if I might somehow be able to damage it, I slid along the bed until I could reach the small lamp on the nightstand. Clicking it to life, I stared at my ten words once more.

CARL
BE CAREFUL
NOTHING IS AS IT SEEMS
A FRIEND

Now, I asked myself, what the hell did that mean? Who could have sent it? Who knew I was coming to Gore? In seconds I had my requisitioned cell phone in my hand and was dialing Tony's number. It didn't even dawn on me that even though he was two time zones away that I probably would be disturbing him. If it had dawned on me I wouldn't have cared. He answered after three rings, snarling:

"Kolchak? What in the name of Jesus, Mary and Joseph could you possibly want already?"

"Tony? How did you know it was me?" I stared dumbly for a second, then asked with hope, "Were you expecting me to call?"

"Why would I be expecting you to call," he demanded. "You never call in unless you want something you can't have. Then you go ahead and take it anyway, leaving me..." I could hear the light bulb switching on over his head.

"What have you done, Kolchak? What are you up to?"

"Tony, wait ..."

"Oh, I can feel the blood starting to boil in my veins. Is this what you want, to kill me in my own home?"

"No, you don't ..."

"My wife—"

"Vincenzo," I shouted, "will you shut up and tell me how you knew I was on the phone?"

"What do you mean?" He asked the question as if I had inquired as to how one ties their shoes. Not waiting for me to continue, he added, "You took a company phone. You took phone #3. That's what it says on my caller ID, Dispatch3. What's wrong with you? Have you been drinking already?"

"No, but it's not a bad idea."

When he growled at me, I told him why I had called. I asked who knew where I was—not what state, but who exactly might know where I was spending the night. "Myself, Slate and Irene" was his answer. He admitted that any number of others could have found out if they had wanted to, but why would they? Normally I would have delighted in throwing a worry up his spine, but I was too worried myself to spread it around.

I told him about Roy and the letter. I read him my ten terse words. I described the essential blank plainness of the paper and its envelope. His world as sour as ever, he said:

"Listen, Carl, to tell the truth, I'd take this thing seriously. I don't think that there's anyone who likes you enough to go to this much trouble for a prank."

"Now wait a minute, Vincenzo, if no one likes me, why does this whoever-it-is want me to be careful? And what's with the X-Files warning? And why not let me know who it is? Why do they have to hide themselves from me?"

We worried over that set of concerns together for a moment. The best we could come up with was that if, and we went to great lengths to make certain that neither one of us was beyond thinking of this situation as an "if" type one yet, that if this weren't a gag, then whoever sent me that note was playing some kind of dangerous game. That they didn't dare sign their name out of fear of blowing their own cover.

I believed Tony when he said he had nothing to do with it. Yes, he's not above a practical joke. But, if it had been him, he would have ended it then and there. My beloved Italian tortoise was not one to risk a reporter on an expense account running around wasting time, and company money, chasing wild geese. I also believed him when he told me he wanted me to call in every day and keep him updated on the situation.

We hung up after that, and I kept sitting on the bed, wondering just what the hell was going on. With nothing better to do, I reviewed my facts as careful as I could. Fact number one: someone sent me a mysterious letter. Fact number two: they were clearly warning me that there was something more to the local murders than anyone knew, and that involvement in this particular story could be dangerous—at least for me, if not everyone. Fact number three: whatever was going on, the murders were most likely just the proverbial tip of the Titanic wrecker, and that most likely they probably were only a signpost pointing to whatever the real story was hidden around here somewhere.

And fact number four: whatever that real story was, it was something so dangerous that someone cautioning me to watch out for myself was so worried about what was going on they didn't dare identify themselves.

And, fact five if you will: whoever my benefactor was, they were good at not identifying themselves. They hadn't hand-written the note. It had been printed out in Courier, a type face so mundane it was in every computer in the known universe. They had centered everything to keep from giving away any stylistic clues. And, they had also avoided all punctuation, most likely for the same reason.

Who could I possibly know, I asked myself several hundred times that evening, who was that clever, that well connected, and that frightened? I could have asked myself several thousand times, but it became obvious quickly I was not going to find any answers that night. Thus I went back over everything Tony and I had said to see if there was anything I had missed.

When I got to the part where he asked me if I'd been drinking, I hit myself in the head with the flat of my hand. Wondering what I was waiting for, I reached inside the larger of my two bags and pulled forth a rather cheap, third class bottle of Scotch. Breaking the seal, I took a long pull straight from the bottle. Coming up for air, I wiped my mouth at the same time with my sleeve, then took another.

I was gifted with no revelations over who might have sent the letter, but I felt better about it. As I hefted the bottle once more, the polite section of my brain reminded me that there were glasses and ice available. I chuckled at how frivolous I can be at times.

After that, I took another deep slug, dropping the bottle's screw cap on the nightstand as if I actually intended to use it again. ●

CHAPTER SIX

I awoke at roughly 8:45 A.M. This was not because I remembered to leave a wake-up call, or out of any overriding sense of duty. Nor is it even approximately my preferred time to arise. Unfortunately, not having eaten in something like eighteen hours, the calories to be garnered from a pint bottle of less-than-interesting Scotch withstanding, it was the growling of my stomach, accompanied by the clarion section ringing in my ears, which forced me awake. I think if either a sneeze or a burp had found their way into the score, the additional sound might well have given Vincenzo an early Christmas present by allowing him to finally write my obituary. Something in the idea of being that generous spurred me to action.

Dragging myself out of bed, it took roughly some six minutes in the bathroom before my reason for pouring so much seasoned varnish down my throat came back to me. I staggered out into the main area of my room, leaving my shorts behind on the floor, so I could look the single sheet of non-descript paper over once more. I wasn't worried; I was reasonably certain I could find my way back to them. I was not so certain I could wait to stare at the annoyingly enigmatic communication.

Sadly, it was still as oblique to me in the morning as it had been the evening before. Tired of standing naked in the no-so-well heated room, staring like an idiot at something I knew held no clues for me, I wandered back to the bathroom. At least I was sitting.

CARL
BE CAREFUL
NOTHING IS AS IT SEEMS
A FRIEND

The damn thing still read the same. It also still meant nothing to me. Continuing to rule my kingdom, I brushed my teeth while staring, ran my brushes through my hair, and did my mouthwash rinse. Finally rising, I had to make a decision. Was I simply going to curl up into a ball and burn my eyeballs out on what could still simply be someone's idea of the gag of the century, or was I going to get to work?

"Be careful," I muttered, reaching for my razor. "Nothing is as it seems." Holding the paper up to the mirror, I showed it to myself, then stared into my eyes as I added:

"Are you telling me, Carl, after all this time, that you need someone to tell you this?"

I had no answer. Of course, it wasn't the message that was bothering me. It was the fact it existed. It was the idea that someone knew I was in town, that they were expecting me, watching for me... and that I didn't know who they were. Suddenly angry with myself, I crumpled the sheet up and threw it in the wastebasket.

Grabbing the complimentary sliver of soap, I unwrapped it, then held it under the hot water for a moment to get both it and my hands wet. Working up a lather with it, I slapped the suds on my face and began to shave. Feeling annoyed with my unreasoned fear, I took my time and did a slick job. Then I wet my hair and brushed it again. I even took out the small pair of scissors that came with my travel bag a dozen years earlier and did what trimming I could.

Working at making myself presentable for the gentry of Gore, West Virginia, before I knew it I found myself suddenly growing angry–angry for getting frightened over essentially nothing. Angry for using nonsense as an excuse to gift myself with a hangover. First day on the streets of a new town, getting ready to introduce myself to a new set of hidebound lawmen, and I was letting the same willful patterns tear me down that had done so so many times in the past.

"Well, not today, Carl," I told the face in the mirror. "For once let's do this right. Let's go out there looking like someone who deserves respect, and let's see if we can't get some."

The face in the mirror gave me an approving grin, as if it liked this new and different idea. There was a twinkle in its eye I recognized, and an overall sardonic flair to its look I knew helped with the ladies, if nothing else. I had somehow managed to pile my hair in just that precise set of layers those truly sophisticated women would call "dreamy." All in all, I believe I was actually pleased with myself.

Then, my eye caught sight of the crumpled ball in the wastebasket. The thing no longer bothered me. After all, I told myself, it wasn't actually bad news. In fact, when I thought about it, all it meant really was that someone was letting me know they were on my side. No one meaning me harm would send me a note like this. No one that knew me would think I could be scared off a story by such a thing; no one that didn't know me would have tried to do so by addressing it "Carl." Nor would they have signed it "A Friend."

I did pull it out of the trash, however. Finding the envelope, I stuffed both in my bag for disposal outside. If there was someone watching me who wasn't on my side, eventually they were going to be sneaking into my room and looking into my things. No sense letting them know that for once someone might be looking over my shoulder for me.

I took a few extra moments brushing down my suit, albeit with my hands, and making myself look as presentable as possible. Then, preparing a mental checklist, I got my pad and pen ready to take down some information from whomever was on the front desk. I would need a place to find an overcoat, the local police, the local newspaper, a good breakfast and the crime scene.

There were several ways to play rolling into a small town, and I had decided that for once, perhaps I wouldn't pack an abundance of belligerence in my utility belt. There was something going on beyond what anyone else knew. This was more than just a murderer on the loose. It was more even than some kind of monster murderer on the loose. The crumpled sheet of eight and a half by eleven in my bag told me that much.

I knew this was going to be a big story, and that the tiny town of Gore, West Virginia, was going to be crawling with additional media before the night was out. If I wanted to be the fat and sassy wordologist who chewed this particular headline burger up and then burped out a report to the world, I was going to have to use the golden bit of extra information that had been deep-throated into my lap to my best advantage.

Camera around my neck, laptop over my shoulder, hatchback keys in hand, I smiled at myself in the larger mirror of the main room and saw that its backward reproduction of me was feeling pretty confident. A degree away from smug, I told the happy guy I saw:

"Looking hot for once."

Then I opened the door, and was slammed in the face by Virginia in early December, finding my previous self-satisfaction disappearing as I remembered exactly *why* that the hot guy in the mirror still needed an overcoat. ●

CHAPTER SEVEN

Roy had been off duty, but the equally attentive and erudite Mel was there in his place. Mel, short for Melvin Abjureen, a short, balding man of Indian (correctly used, as in New Delhi) heritage, proved to be the proprietor of my current residence. And if anything, as owner of the establishment, Mel was even more interested in his patrons and their well-being than Roy had been. In only a matter of minutes, maintaining the largest of smiles Mel clearly pinpointed for me all the locations I had need of that day. He also gave me the directions to them all in a kind of figure eight pattern which allowed me to find them in the most efficient manner.

For instance, the local sheriff's office might have been the closest thing to us, but what kind of sense did it make for me to stumble into it hungry and shivering? That hardly befit the new image I was trying to create for myself that morning. So, even though it meant driving past two of my destinations, the first place Mel sent me was to Hibbel's Five & Dime. The place did a landmark business in used clothes, he told me, but they always fixed up anything they put out for sale. He pointed to the shirt he was wearing that day with pride, saying:

"I am telling you now, this is a most fine shirt, and I found it at Hibbel's, and five more just like it the same day, and every one of them I purchased for under a dollar. This is the place for you, my friend."

Figuring even the *Dispatch* could afford Hibbel's, I followed Mel's directions and got myself to the Five & Dime posthaste. Not wanting to waste any more daylight, not with the sun doling less of it out every day, I looked for someone who might be able to come to my aid. I must have looked particularly in need of assistance, for the next person who came through the door, a quite attractive younger woman, almost immediately said to me:

"Gracious, you poor dear, what are you doing out today with just a suit coat on? You'll catch your death."

She was a well-shaped blonde, possessing dark brown eyes, a modest nose, thin, nicely-formed lips, a long neck and a friendly disposition toward helpless reporters—pretty much my favorite type of female to be assisted by.

"Well," I said, hoping to God I hadn't used up all my charm for the day on Mel, "it's like this ..."

As quickly as I could, I explained my situation to her, begging her in the way all men have begged for assistance when they really had something else on their minds since those sad days when it was decided a club to the head was gauche. My savior's name turned out to be LuAnn Hildebergen. She was recently divorced, a newly-arrived transplant who had come to the area to take a research job at the local state college, and the type of woman who adored any excuse to dress a man.

I soon found myself trying on a variety of coats, all chosen with care to protect my big city image. LuAnn claimed to find it charming that I would confide my expense account needs to her, and while she sighed wistfully over the thought of living where no one needed a top-to-bottom weather shield, she managed to find a heavy natural leather jacket lined with actual wool which couldn't have been toastier if it came with a built-in campfire. It even possessed that wonderfully old-fashioned pocket design which allowed one to slide their hand behind the overcoat pocket through a special slit and reach inside to their inner pockets.

When I marveled at its insanely reasonable price, wondering if I was being done some remarkable favor, or being hustled in some way I could not discern, LuAnn refused to allow a doubt to linger in my mind. Summoning the owner of the shop, a pleasant, middle-aged woman with a disposition as sweet as a perfectly picked pineapple, she asked about the price. LuAnn's question received a shower of laughter in response.

I shrugged in honest helplessness, a motion to which my shining angel made motions of agreement. Her outburst finally contained, the store owner told us in between several outbursts of the giggles:

"Oh, hon, no—don't you worry about that. It's a good coat. You can see that. Truth is, we did have it marked a lot higher at first, but we couldn't sell it."

"Too steep for the locals," I hazarded, not trying to be insulting, simply not knowing where else to go. The owner waved her hands in front of her face as if trying to dry her nail polish, telling us:

"No, no. You know we sell a lot of old pieces here, right?" We both nodded. "And you saw the tag, you know this was a used piece, right?" LuAnn and I nodded in unison once more, both of us wondering where we were being lead. Her voice dropping to a whisper, the store owner confided:

"Well, it might be a nice coat, but no one wanted it because it was just too recognizable. People 'round here don't much like the old owner."

"Well," I said, "I don't know him, and I don't want you to tell me about him, either."

"Whatever you say, hon," the owner responded. "But, if I can ask, why not?" Admiring how I looked in what was soon to become my new coat in the mirror, I answered:

"Because, if I began to share the local opinion of this fellow, I might be forced to put back this wonderful coat. And I wouldn't want to do that."

"Oh, you certainly wouldn't," answered the owner.

"And you wouldn't want me to, would you?"

"Oh, Heavens, no," she giggled helplessly.

I turned from side to side, looking at myself in the three-side mirror, happiness seeping into every pour as I enjoyed being truly warm for the first time since I'd arrived in the state. Having LuAnn giving me admiring looks did not hurt my general outlook on life, either. Not able to imagine ever slipping the coat off again, I found myself not worried about anything except how far it was to the diner Mel had chosen for me. The store owner and LuAnn both agreed with his choice as my *Dispatch* credit card was processed.

I asked LuAnn if it would be too forward for a lowly newshound to ask a respectable college researcher to join him for breakfast. She replied, smiling in a way that warmed me more thoroughly than my wonderful new coat, telling me that I wasn't being forward at all, but that she unfortunately had to shop and run. She did hand me her business card, however, letting me know that college researchers were known to eat dinner on occasion as well. Her smile undiminished, she added:

"Gracious, now that wasn't too forward of me, was it?"

"Being worse than a Yankee," I answered, "being a Yankee who now lives in California, I'm sure I wouldn't have the faintest idea of what's proper in this world anymore. But, I will add that if it's a certain Ms. Hildebergen whose manners have been brought into question, then I'd have to say 'no,' I can't imagine it was too forward at all."

She smiled at me again, and I nodded in return, asking her what time college researchers like to dine. She told me, then pointed a few doors up and across the street to a semi-rough looking diner. The single plank sign nailed above the door reading "LET LARRY FEED YA" in bold yellow letters identified it as Mel's favorite eatery in town.

"They make a good breakfast," she said, "but we might want to dine somewhere less ... 'rustic' tonight."

"You have shielded my fragile shell against nature herself, dear lady," I told her. "With such strength as you have given me, how could I be anything but your humble servant, and take you any place except the one you deem most suitable?"

"I do declare," LuAnn said in a mock Southern Belle voice, "They're coming up with a surprisingly more well-mannered brand of Yankee these days."

Feeling ever so gallant, I bowed, and then kissed her hand, giving her the tiniest of waves as I walked out into the street. After that I simply turned in the direction she had pointed and headed for the diner. For once I was feeling pretty good about myself. Hot case, hot coat, hot date—yes, for roughly ninety-five seconds I was actually enjoying life for a change. Then, I slipped my hand into my inner pocket and felt the letter and envelope I had rescued from the trash can—the ones I had been too frightened to leave behind.

It's amazing how the slightest bit of paranoia can ruin a perfectly good day. ●

CHAPTER EIGHT

The Larry of the yellow-lettered LET LARRY FEED YA turned out to be an aging hippy who wasn't so much into granola and saving the whales as he was getting everyone to simply chill out and make more peace than war. Tall as your average door, but only as wide as a broom, the diner's proprietor was a stick of a man whose idea of commerce was to serve big plates filled with hot, simple food. He was also balding, gap-toothed and extremely pleasant, and by the way he piled his platters even less worried about the plight of hogs, chickens and cows as he was that of the whales.

Breakfast was the Special, "Larry's Li'l Plate of Heaven," a trayful of goodness which consisted of two eggs, toast, hash browns, bacon, sausage and two pancakes, with grapefruit juice and coffee with which to wash it down. None of it was pre-packaged, not even the butter. Well, all right, the maple syrup came from some soulless conglomerate on the outside, but Larry even squeezed his own juice. It was the perfect meal for a man mending a hangover, and Larry himself was just topping my coffee off for a second time when an officer of the law approached my table.

"Good mornin'," he said, politely enough that I didn't automatically start searching for my soap box, either to climb on top of or to crawl under. "You the reporter, Carl Kolchak?"

"Most days," I answered, hoping the automatic flippancy in my tone wouldn't work the wonders it does for me with most lawmen. "Something wrong, officer?"

"I'm Will Jeeter," he announced with a certain likable modesty, "I'm the sheriff around here. I was told you were lookin' for me."

"Why yes, sheriff, I was going to be stopping by your office right after Larry here stopped treating me like a king."

"Then I'd never meet you," he said, giving the proprietor a wink, "'cause Larry don't never stop treatin' folks like royalty, do you, Larr?"

"I toil for the public ceaselessly, as if charged to it from above," he responded, grabbing a cup from another table and filling it to the brim for Jeeter. Handing it to the officer, he added: "Allow me to demonstrate."

The sheriff thanked him politely, taking a deep sip then allowing a satisfied sigh to escape his lips. Larry nodded in appreciation, then moved back just far enough to listen in on our conversation. Paying him no mind, Jeeter turned to me, cup in hand, and asked:

"Mind if I join you? I feel foolish standin', especially with the cup and all..."

"Heavens, sheriff," I said honestly, warming to Jeeter easily enough. "Forgive me. Please, sit, sit. Join me."

The sheriff thanked me and eased into the chair opposite mine. His movements were slow, studied. He was a middle-aged man, maybe nine, ten years my senior, but he seemed solid enough to handle his job. His shoulders were wide; his jaw was a heavy, protruding thing, which might have stood out more if the green of his eyes didn't so completely capture your attention. When he took off his official cap, his full head of hair proved to be a sandy kind of brown that kept drawing your attention upward until you forgot the chin. He would have made a swell character actor if he hadn't become a lawman.

"So, sheriff, most towns I go to someone usually drags me down to the station to read me one type of riot act or another. And, I must admit, from the look on your face as you came up to the table, I thought you were coming to run me out of town."

The lawman looked at me strangely, as if he didn't understand, and then suddenly started to laugh. When I inquired as to what the joke was, he told me:

"Sorry about the scowl; that wasn't aimed at you. I was lookin' at your coat. I see you've been over to the Thrift."

The sheriff's humor was so genuine I had to grin myself. Taking a sip of my fresh-squeezed grapefruit juice, a true delicacy I was thoroughly enjoying, I smacked my lips, then glanced over at my new coat, saying:

"I heard the old owner of this thing wasn't all that popular. Now I'm thinking he must have been a real peach."

"Oh, yeah," Jeeter answered slowly. "That's one word for him."

"Well, you probably didn't come here to discuss my coat, so perhaps I should let you get down to business. I'm certain you can understand that like anyone else, having the police show up at the breakfast table has got me wondering to what do I owe the honor of such personal attention?"

"Don't worry, Mr. Kolchak. There's nothin' serious. I was over to the motel this morning, and Mel told me to expect you after you did your shoppin' and had breakfast. I figured, any excuse for a chance to snag a cup of Larry's coffee ..."

"Well, sir," I said, willing to believe him for the moment, "as an out-of-town newsman, I make a point of stopping in with the local authorities, especially when we're talking about asking for permission to tour homicide sites. So, should we continue this at your office, or ..."

Jeeter put up his hand to cut me off. It wasn't a bullying kind of I'll-do-the-talking motion you get out of many behind a badge, but a friendlier, no-need-for-that kind of gesture that relaxed me even further.

"There's nothin' down there we need that we don't already have here, and the coffee's a darn sight better. If you don't mind, Mr. Kolchak... I am sayin' that right, ain't I ..."

I nodded my head a couple of short bobs to indicate he was hitting all syllables fine. He gave me a slight smile and a nod of his own, then continued, saying:

"Good, good. No, if you could just give me the usual, a little background on you and your outlet, how long you expect to be here, what you want to know, where you want to go... I'm sure you know the routine better than I do."

I smiled back, realizing that sheriff Will Jeeter was one of the most disarming men I'd ever met. Picking up my last piece of toast, I wrapped it around a half a sausage link and most of a piece of bacon. Poising it to take a bite, I assured him I did know the routine, noticing that my usual defensive sarcasm had almost completely drained from my tone. As I bit down and started to chew, he took another long pull from his coffee cup, then said:

"I mean, I'll be honest with you, as you might guess, we don't get a lotta big city types rollin' through Gore askin' questions. Mel said you seemed like an okay guy. Said his nightman thinks you can take a joke, anyway. So really, if you wouldn't mind, I'd just like to get a feel from you, if you don't mind, that is, of what I can expect the next couple of days, when CBS and *Newsweek* and all those other boys start showin' up."

I told him everything he wanted to know, and even threw in a few extras. With every word Jeeter continued to impress me as a decent sort who shortly might be in for more than he'd ever bargained for. I gave him some tips on the kinds of things reporters have been known to do to get around the authorities, the kinds of swindles that left lawmen looking stupid, their towns embarrassed, and their citizens thinking maybe someone else needed a chance to look good in a uniform.

Some might think I was betraying my own kind, but the way I saw it, Jeeter was one of the few policemen I'd ever met who didn't start out by trying to impress upon me what a tough guy he was. Considering how many of my own had tried to metaphorically cut my throat over the years for a couple lousy extra inches of play, I figured being up front and honest with someone who gave every appearance of doing the same for me was not something that was going to hurt me any.

"So, Mr. Kolchak," the sheriff asked, working on his second cup of coffee at that point, as well as a Danish I had insisted he allow me to put on the *Dispatch's* expense account, "what made your paper pick you for this assignment? L.A. to V.A. this time of year... somebody there not like you?"

I chuckled. Larry did as well.

"Seems there's someone everywhere that doesn't like me," I told him, getting another smile out of the proprietor as well, "but at our rag, I'm pretty much the best guy to send when there's blood on things. We'rpretty much an entertainment outlet, and yes, I know it's a sad commentary on this world of ours that murder has become entertainment, but ..."

I spread my hands wide to indicate I had no explanation for that one. Jeeter nodded, saying:

"Oh, hell, that kind of thing's older than the Romans. We don't let folks gather round pits and watch dogs rip up bears, or each other, anymore, or fightin' birds... bullfights, nuthin'. On the one hand we act like we're all civilized, but on the other you just try and keep those civilized types who make all the rules about what's proper and what's not from stickin' their head out and gawkin' at a road accident."

"He's right, Carl," said Larry, finally becoming an active participant in the conversation. "People who want to be in charge, I don't care if it's your local block association, the PTA or the Pentagon, the ones who *want* to run things, you know who I mean, the ones who really *need* to be in charge, those are the people you've got to watch out for. The wrong thinking a lot of my generation made was in not realizing, okay—yeah—you need all that stuff, from the PTA to the Pentagon, and yeah, you're hearing me right; the long-haired freak is defending a country's right to keep an army. But, what I'm saying is you've got to be goddamned careful about just who you let run these damn things."

"Especially the PTA," said Jeeter wryly. Larry laughed out loud, and I knew I was suddenly privy to some private local humor.

"Gentlemen," I said, feeling a unity I hadn't in quite some time. "The two of you make me wonder if I haven't somehow found my long-lost brothers. No Polish blood in either of your backgrounds, is there?"

Both men laughed, and for the first time in a longer span than I could remember, I actually did feel as if I were home. Since I had arrived after the breakfast crowd and before the lunch set, Larry had no one else to worry about at the moment and so finally pulled up his own chair, saying it made it easier than walking back and forth to pour us coffee. Setting the pot in the middle of the table, he told us to pour our "own damn coffee," and sat back to light up a cigarette.

For a second my eyes went wide at such a sight, and then my memory kicked in and reminded me that in some parts of America people were still allowed to go to hell in their own ways as long as they weren't hurting anyone else. He and Jeeter both chuckled at my reaction, and I just smiled.

As we all worked on finishing off the pot in the center of the table, I went back to telling the sheriff why I'd been chosen to come to Gore. I gave him some of my background from the old days covering the crime beat in New York and Chicago. Then I hinted at my "specialty niche" as the guy they sent out to cover the occasional "strange" case. I didn't go into details, not wanting to ruin their good opinion of me. It turned out there was no need for me to be coy. Larry stared at me for a moment, and then starting snapping his fingers, saying:

"Kolchak, Kolchak, Carl Kolchak... you know, when you said that stuff about strange cases and all, that's ringing a bell... something I saw on the internet, now what was that? Com'on, Carl, help me out here ..."

It didn't take too long before Larry pieced together exactly which "Carl Kolchak" I was. As I hid my face behind my hand, wondering how long it would be before the sheriff started trying to find a way to take me on a tour of the town limits, Larry began to rattle off everything he could remember from several websites that mentioned my work prominently. The proprietor of LET LARRY FEED YA was a major UFO enthusiast, to whom apparently I was something of a minor celebrity.

To my amazement, Jeeter not only didn't do an about-face on me, but began to ask questions about things I might have seen in the past which could relate to what he was up against. I told him that I didn't have any particular theories, that indeed I liked to keep the supernatural and the like out of things until it was unavoidable. I also volunteered to share any information with him I thought might be helpful after I'd started looking over the crime scenes. Will Jeeter seemed like a decent fellow to me, and I couldn't see a thing wrong with helping him out—especially if it made my own job that much easier.

He was in the process of thanking me when his radio went off. Immediately the sheriff stood and headed for the front door. Larry started gathering our dishes, cups and the such, telling me:

"He'll be back. He just can't get reception in here. Roof must have a layer of tin or lead or something in it. Cell phones don't work in here, either."

Larry's prediction had been on the money. The sheriff returned in less than a minute. In that time, however, his demeanor had changed radically. Indeed, the new look on his face, the way he was carrying himself, I wondered if someone hadn't given him orders to direct me toward the nearest rail, and to hold me there until the tar and feather committees could rendezvous with us.

"Carl," he said, in a voice so dark I almost had to wonder if he were the same human being who had walked out the door. "How'd you like to take a ride with me?" Working to keep the sudden apprehension I was feeling from my voice, I asked:

"Where to, sheriff?"

"Rafe Holister's farm," he answered quietly, his voice almost a whisper. "It's just outside of town. Seems there's been another murder."

A chill settled in the air around us that no amount of leather and wool was going to dismiss. Getting to my feet, my voice unable to reach a volume any louder that Jeeter's, I asked:

"Does it look like the same killer?"

"There were some differences." Fumbling for my wallet, I spilled some money on the table, not remembering the company's expense card, just trying to get myself ready to move as the sheriff told me, "this time it was an entire family. Mother, father, three kids... grandparents... one madien aunt..."

There was a hard line of ice in Jeeter's voice, a cold but brittle anger that let me know he was barely holding it together. Maybe they were people he knew too well for him to accept what had happened. Maybe it was just too much, the thought that whatever was out there, it now looked like perhaps instead of simply moving through his community, it was settling down for a long winter's visit. Maybe he felt as if it might not have happened if he hadn't been wasting time drinking coffee with me.

A dozen other theories raced through my head as well, then the sheriff finished his sentence, and I knew what it was that had pushed him to the edge.

"And this time," he growled darkly, "this time all the pieces weren't left behind." ●

CHAPTER NINE

From the road, Rafe Holister's place looked like any other typical farm. It did not pretend to be in touch with the carefully groomed elegance of Rockwell's Americana. It was merely a working spread of acres one family had stayed upon for six generations. It was simple, well-cared for, and it was theirs. Except that now, there was no "they" to lay claim to it anymore. Something in the night had seen to that.

Something with fangs far larger than I had yet imagined—than I had found in any of my previous bizarre encounters. Something with claws that must have been the size of hammers. The work they did supported the thought that they must be ruthless, terrible things—massive and overwhelmingly destructive—powered by hands that could crush bone and knot metal. And though I might have wished that some of my description were only hyperbole, across all of the Holister farm, there was ample, terrible evidence to support my theories.

"So, tell me, Carl, and tell me honest ..."

The grandparents must have been taking the night air on the front porch. Sitting on the wooden swing, braving the early December evening so they could enjoy one another's intimate company, simply watching the stars together, the sound of the gently moving chains covering any movement—sounds of approach also not heard by Wendel Halford, nor the still unidentified soul found behind Gore Center Village. Like those two unfortunates, the elder Holisters had been rendered into shamefully tiny fragments, strewn about the front of the house like so much scarlet confetti. They, also like the previous two victims, had merely been slaughtered and dismembered, their blood splattered along the length of the porch, across the windows, over the bushes and the flower beds already turned for the winter to come.

"This like anything you've ever seen before?"

I shook my head numbly. Even though on the one hand I had already taken a score of pictures, I had done so quietly, respectfully. It's true that I've been witness to a lot in my time. In all honesty, I'd seen gang-slayings in Chicago which could match the brutality of the Holister's front porch. I was willing to bet, however, that Sheriff Jeeter had never seen anything like what we were witnessing together—not even in his worst nightmares. On the other hand, I was also willing to wager that we hadn't seen anything yet.

"No," I finally muttered, "nothing like this. Criminals paying back other criminals, trying to make a point. But...," my eyes settled on grandma's crushed skull, one eye intact, one ruined, and shuddered slightly as I simply repeated myself, "no. Nothing, nothing like this."

As we came closer to the front of the house, the front door began to swing open. The action made both of us jump, but the figure coming through the door proved to be one Allen Campbell, the deputy sheriff who had called Jeeter in the first place. His pace slow and jerky, arms dangling useless at his sides, he looked like a man on the verge of collapse.

"Hey, Sheriff," he said weakly. He made a feeble salute, his hand trembling badly as he did so. His face was ashen, drained of color. His eyes were blood-shot, swollen and burning. I had no doubt whatsoever there was a pool of breakfast steaming somewhere on the property that used to belong to deputy Campbell.

In the city, any big city, it would be a contest to see if the media or the police could make the sickest comments. I could hear the opening zingers forming in my mind. There, however, with men who were not used to such callousness, who had never needed to develop such shells, the regular body bag one-liners not only seemed disrespectful, they seemed shocking. Vulgar.

"What do we have inside?"

"It's horrible, sheriff," answered the deputy, his voice edged with fright and confusion. Unconsciously leaning against the outside wall of the house, Campbell slid downward, smearing the thick coating of blood there. He either was too far into shock to realize what he was doing, or he simply had lost the ability to care.

"It's just horrible."

"How'd you come to be here," asked Jeeter, steeling himself for the moment when he would enter the house. "Does anybody else know about this yet?"

"I, I... I don't think anyone else knows. I came out on a disturbance call. Neighbors said Holister's dogs were acting crazy. When I got here, they were running in circles in the yard, barking their fool heads off. Two of them, anyway. The others..."

As his voice trailed off his lower jaw began to quiver as if there was actually something remaining in his stomach to be expelled. The deputy pointed inside, but stood sideways, barring our path. It was plain to see he was telling us where the other dogs were, but that he wasn't telling us to go inside.

"What about the rest of Rafe's pack, Allen? Why were they inside?"

"It's hard to tell, but... I think, I think they were, were trying to protect the kids. The little ones... I mean, their bodies, they, they ..."

And then, the tears finally started to flow. Allen Campbell buried his face in his duty gloves and began to sob. Neither Jeeter nor I tried to stop him. The deputy appeared at best to be twenty-four. He had the look of a former high school football star—the local boy all the pretty girls swooned over in public and the less pretty ones dreamed about in private. Just another all-American kid playing grown-up in a world where protecting people from the truth was job one. Tall and rugged, and far too young to be prepared for the charnel nightmare he had stumbled upon at Rafe Holister's, Campbell had been slammed full in the throat with the truth that morning, and it had cut him off at the knees and left him weak and blubbering.

The rest of the story unfolded slowly as the deputy worked to pull himself together. Campbell steadied himself somewhat finally by sitting on the top step there on the front porch. Tears continued to flow down his face, many collecting in his thin, feathery moustache, turning to ice. When asked, he told the sheriff that, yes, he had put in a call to the county coroner. Wiping his eyes so he could consult his watch, he estimated that we could expect to be joined by him within a half an hour. Then, slowly, quietly, Campbell began to describe all that he had witnessed inside.

I took a peek through the open front door. What little I could see backed up the deputy's description one hundred percent. The rest of the family looked to have been slaughtered in exactly the manner described in the previous two murders, exactly as were the grandparents scattered up and down the porch and across the front lawn—limbs strewn everywhere, faces ripped off skulls, blood splattered up the front wall of the house, across the roof of the porch's awning, smeared up and down its pillars.

Vital organs had been torn free from the bodies, tossed with such force against walls and furniture they had stuck to or become embedded within that which they struck. And, this time, they had also been eaten.

"I, I can't say for sure, Will, I mean, I mean ..."

"Don't rush things, Al," the sheriff told his man, trying as best he could to help the deputy keep it together even while he himself felt like falling apart. "Just take it easy. One step at a time. No one expects you to do the coroner's job. Just tell me what you can."

I was dying to get inside, but understood the realities. This was a major crime scene. Most likely the biggest one in the history of the town. If Will Jeeter's mind wasn't rushing forward that far yet, running over the implications of what was to come, mine certainly was.

This kind of homicide, this was more than just news, this was going to end up being ***international*** news. Yes, it was true that serial killers and mass murderers had long since ceased to be the automatic ratings grab they used to be. Back in the fifties and sixties, when the concept was barely even understood by the general public, the simple exploits of an Ed Gein, or a Charles Starkweather could keep the wires burning from one end of the country to the other for months. Nowadays, however, people were too easily bored to care about anything as run-of-the-mill as a simple serial killer.

Not only had there been too many of them in real life, but art had rushed in to copy them to the point where the idea was boring. There had been far too many novels, too many movies made about them. Like vampires, the serial killer had come full circle in the public's imagination to where they didn't even make interesting villains anymore. I remember years ago in my younger days when the film "Silence of the Lambs" came out. It shocked the world—frightened everyone. After only two sequels, however, the cannibal murderer star of the series ended up outwitting the police, and running away with the FBI officer with whom he matched wits in the first film. The big twist was her fragile beauty becoming his reward for being such a clever boy.

I shuddered for a moment, not for the carnage and violence all about me, but for how much further the monstrousness of it was going to desensitize the already supremely jaded American public. Staring at the crazed smears of blood running across the front of the Holister home, one thing I knew for certain was that this boy wasn't going to bore people. Not in the least. Whether he meant to be or not, this monster was media savvy, and he was about to be focused with enough attention to keep three rock bands and six heiresses happy.

The killer had caught the nation's interest with his first murder in two ways. First off, he left no clues, not a single mote for the crime scene investigation boys and girls to study. Having their protectors stumped is just the kind of thing that seems to impress the chuckleheaded public these days. Secondly, this guy didn't just kill his victims, he annihilated them. That was enough to catch the bored, limp masses for another evening. How Morgan Slate had seen this all coming, I had no idea, of course, but my hat was off to him. The slaughter of the Holister family was going to enflame the world.

I could afford to show my respects and stay out of the crime scene for the moment. After all, for all intents and purposes, I had an exclusive. Once the county coroner was finished with the place, it would be my turn. I would email my pictures and the first of my articles off to California, and then while they jumped to the task of terrifying the world, I would escort the lovely LuAnn to some fine restaurant, where with luck they might even have dancing. And after all that eating, drinking, and close contact, who knew what might happen?

And all around us, people would be locking their doors, bolting their shutters, cleaning their guns and lying awake in the dark listening for footsteps which apparently no one could hear. And it would be my words creating all the havoc. Oh, and don't think, dear readers, that I give myself too much credit–that it's all the killer's fault, and that I'm punishing myself needlessly. For, where I thank you for the kindness, I must protest. You see, there are ways I could word my article that day, and all the ones I would file in the days to come, which could inform and calm at the same time. But, no publisher is interested in printing copy like that.

Nor are any reporters, including yours truly, interested in turning copy like that in to our publishers. Like the rest of you, we're driven to keep our jobs by turning in ever-higher levels of performance. Believe me, I would be doing everything I could to scare the ever-loving daylights out of everyone I could.

Ironically, little did I know I was going to be getting all the help I could ever want before I knew it. ●

CHAPTER TEN

Thomas Wiffalon, the local coroner, was a grizzled, old-time crewcut of a man, one with multiple papers, plastic gloves and various other bits of apparatus sticking out of all his pockets. He might have moved slowly, wheezing while he did so, but he worked quickly and efficiently, keeping his own council as he moved across the slaughterhouse which was the Holister property. When we were introduced, his only question to me was:

"You know how to conduct yourself around a crime scene?"

"Stay in your footsteps," I answered, "stay out of any room you haven't been in or are still in, keep my mouth shut until you ask me if I have any questions?" He eyeballed me for a moment, then threw me the keys to his car, saying:

"There's a large gray metal case in the trunk. Go get it. Knock on the front door when you get back. I'll tell you when to come in."

I did as I was told, recognizing a continent-sized break when it's handed to me. Wiffalon was coroner for the entire county. That meant checking into and signing off on every single death for a fairly large section of territory—and not just the people. His kind of job in that kind of area meant any large mammals, as well. Cows, horses, hogs, et cetera, that died other than under the butcher's blade had to be inspected, cause of death had to be determined, and it all had to be signed off on by him like any other mysterious death. It was how modern farming communities survived plagues. Remember Mad Cow Disease? It was someone like Wiffalon who caught it before it took out too many of us.

As only one man with that much ground to cover, I figured the coroner had probably made a science of studying those he found at a scene, learning how to size them up quickly so he could press one of them into service. He was old and, as I found out, his large gray metal case was extremely heavy. Still, only the world's stupidest reporter would have turned down the chance he was offering. And since Vincenzo had sent myself and not Updyke, Wiffalon got all the service the fourth estate could muster.

The mother and aunt had died in the living room. Nearly everything within the once neatly appointed room had been destroyed, but oddly enough the television set was still on. Wiffalon's efficient, careful study revealed the women were snacking on oranges which they had peeled while watching their program. What they had been watching was left to the imagination. The fact that the television was still running, however, actually added a disturbing note to the grisly scene. All about the room, the body parts and fluids of the two women had been hurled across everything. Afterward, the furnishings, the books in the book case, the family nick-nacks, et cetera, all had been smashed—pulverized. All but the television.

There, in the middle of all that bloody chaos, the idiot box sat serenely, disgorging a soap opera at us, undamaged and unblemished save for a single drop of blood which had found its way to the front of the picture tube. It clung there, a muddy dried brown spot, tiny, but not insignificant. It was simply a quiet reminder of life, surrounded by blaring fantasy. Still, it focused my attention, made the set stick in my mind.

Dragging his metal box, I followed Wiffalon from room to room. We found the remains of the father and his oldest daughter in a side room which could only have been his den and office. As Wiffalon reconstructed things, Dad had been helping his little girl with her homework, and then when they heard screams from the front, he had hurried to unlock his gun cabinet and arm himself. The shotgun he had chosen had been used to impale him to the wall. His head and most of his chest were missing.

The daughter had attempted to hide under her father's desk. She had been dragged out from under it just as far as was necessary so she could be torn in half. Wiffalon figured her for sixteen. Still Daddy's little sweetheart. Most likely still thinking of him as the greatest man in the world. Kind and strong and loving. The one man who would always protect her.

Or at least try.

The other children, and most of the missing dogs, we found upstairs. The dogs could only have been trying to protect the two little ones, most likely asleep, when whatever had lumbered across the Holister farm had begun its rampage. I will admit, even I had to take a pause here. Unlike Campbell, at least I had Wiffalon to prepare me:

"City boy," he said as he exited from the children's room, "you've got yourself a strong constitution—yes?" When I nodded noncommittally, he told me, "you'll need it in there. Just because you can wear that coat without tossing breakfast doesn't mean you're ready for everything this world has to offer."

I was really beginning to wonder who my overcoat's previous owner was. Knowing then was not the time to start asking, I simply affirmed that I thought I'd be all right. Wiffalon nodded, cautioning me as I headed for the door:

"I suggest a deep breath before going in."

He was not referring to odor. The murders were too recent for decay, especially considering the cold of the season. Yes, the heat was still on in the house, but with so many doors and windows shattered, the place was practically an ice box. Besides, Wiffalon would have supplied us all with carbon filter masks, or at least had us all light up cigars, if there was a stench building. But no, sadly, he was not referring to odor.

The children had been roughly two and six. I was taking the coroner's word on that. There was no way for a civilian to even begin to hazard a guess from the remains. The two children had been ripped into pieces, as had the defending pooches, but here the killer had begun to feed again. Even I could spot the bite marks. And, after dinner, our madman had squashed the majority of the remains together, human and canine, within the crib. After that he had hammered at them with his fists until everything had been splintered.

I almost wished for cheap horror movie mood music somewhere in the background. The tackiness of it, the ordinariness of such noise would have pressed the right buttons to bring my mind a bit of relief. But no, nothing like that was in the offing. This was no fiction—this was here, in front of me, daring me to look away. This was cold and brutal murder, bloody insane death to be viewed through tears and a haze of one's own breath.

Something got to me in the kids' room, something that fed on the savage loneliness of all men sooner or later. It clawed up out of the box I'd locked it within years earlier, when thoughts of ever finding the right woman, of settling down, having a real life, kids, a dog, a house with a driveway, a lawn to take care of, all of that crap, any of it, had finally been disposed of by bitter reality. Maybe it was as simple as just having made my piece with reaching middle age recently, but whatever released the hounds of despair within my mind, I felt an anger over what had been done to the children I could not rationalize.

Or escape.

"Don't let it get to you, son."

I wheeled, startled by Wiffalon's words and his hand on my shoulder. I had forgotten him, forgotten my job, where I was, forgotten everything for a moment, lost in a grim shadow of despair blotting the light of hope from my soul. It was melodramatic and it was self-indulgent and it was stupid, but it's what I was feeling and the coroner knew it.

"Not married, are you," he asked. When I shook my head, manfully attempting to pull myself together, he added, "Yeah, neither am I. Let's get out of here—unless you ..."

There was no "unless" for me. I stopped him in mid-sentence, letting him know I had enough for a novel, let alone an article. As we headed downstairs to rejoin the sheriff and his deputy, I told Wiffalon I'd like to talk to him about the previous murder when he had the time. He told me that would be no problem, but he answered absently, his mind somewhere else. As we exited out onto the front porch, he let it be known what he was thinking.

Wiffalon had something of a nose for blood. The man knew his job, and wasn't disturbed by it even when distributed lavishly the way Jeeter and Campbell had been. I, of course, could barely contain my glee at having numerous bodies to photograph, frightened lawmen to interview, and a crusty old character with a forensics degree to add pithy comments to my copy for the day. But, just because the degree of trauma I reached didn't come close to that achieved by the sheriff's department did not mean I was in a class with Wiffalon. Not by a long shot.

As we rejoined the lawmen, the first thing he did was to ask if anyone had tended to the family's livestock. When the three of us just stared at him, the coroner barked:

"Pigs, chickens, cows—ever hear of such things? Ever know them to be found on a farm? Think they might be hungry right about now, let alone need access to the yard?" As Campbell rose to head off to the barns, Wiffalon suggested the sheriff take his place. As Jeeter moved off toward the barn, the coroner pulled a flask from his gray metal case. Unscrewing the cap, he handed it first to the deputy, telling him to take a slug.

"Oh, thanks, but I'm, you know, on duty and all. I can't really..."

"Just take a swallow, you pinhead. You're going to need it."

Wiffalon's growl had been so intense the youngster did as told without further hesitation. He handed it to me, sensing I wasn't a man who needed coaxing in such matters. As I knocked back a couple of fingers of what turned out to be an acceptable blend of rye, he said off-handedly:

"Either of you hear any animal noises while we've been here?" Campbell and I gave the question some thought, then both answered in the negative. Finishing his own long pull on his flask, the coroner said:

"Yeah, me neither. That seem strange to you? A farm where none of the animals make noise?"

Will Jeeter was just throwing open the barn door as it hit me what he was going to find inside. •

CHAPTER ELEVEN

The rest of the day became something of a nightmare for sheriff Jeeter. As Wiffalon had expected, the livestock which had once been a healthy part of the Holister family income was now simply so much slaughtered meat. The barn was such a tangle of limbs and heads, organs and bones, awash in such a nightmarish quantity of blood, that the sight of it was practically more than the human mind could handle.

Jeeter was a friendly man, but amiability could only be stretched so far. I offered to catch a ride back into town with the coroner, taking responsibility for transporting me back there out of his hands. He asked that the name of the family be kept from my article, and that the pictures not reveal things like street signs or numbers. Or that I show the entire house clearly enough that it could be identified. And that I use a bit of discretion with the gruesome content of the interior photographs.

As the sheriff haltingly piled on request after request, I let him know he had nothing to worry about from me. As we shook hands, he told me:

"Keep it that way, and I guarantee you that the rest of your brethren who show up will have to deal with you to get their photos, and a hell of a lot of their content. I've already put Allen to draggin' a few of our regulars into service."

"Regulars?"

"Temporary deputies," he answered. "This farm is going to be off-limits until further notice. I'm goin' to need more people. From what you tell me, a lot more." I nodded. I knew my kind. He was right. After a handful of silent seconds, he added quietly:

"After what we've seen today, make that a hell of a lot more."

I nodded again. There was nothing worth saying. The man was right. And sadly, in the pit of my stomach I had a feeling he had no idea exactly how right he was.

While Jeeter and Campbell attended to the Holister place, I rode back into Gore with Wiffalon. The coroner gave me all he could from memory on the John Doe case from behind Gore Center Village. I taped every precious word, getting a few choice quotes from the man on both crime scenes. Knowing I could easily crib whatever I needed about the original Wendel Halford murder from the papers I'd bought, I was all smiles by the time we made it back to town.

I offered to buy Wiffalon lunch, but he begged off, replying that he had too much to do. I was not there that morning to study sand, however. What I wanted was a look at those others who might be there to study sand. I had the feeling he didn't want to become indebted to the press, but I couldn't have cared less. He had already given me an astounding lead on the rest of the world. I was an e-mail away from world wide fame—the good kind for once.

He let me off at my motel. I checked at the front desk for messages and then went straight to my room. I set to work with such immediacy that I was half finished with the first draft of my article before I realized I'd never taken off my coat. Considering it good luck I left it on until I was done. In less than two hours I had completed three separate pieces which I e-mailed back to the *Dispatch* as they were finished.

My company cell phone started ringing less than five minutes after I sent the first. I chose not to hear it. In less time the motel room phone started to jangle as well. I found it less easy to ignore. Picking it up, I shouted:

"Leave me alone. I'm winning my Pulitzer."

"Carl, Carl!" Vincenzo's voice was glowing. Astounded. "Don't hang up!"

"Speak. And make it quick."

"Just tell me, all verified? No speculation? No imagination? Your own eyes laid on everything—just as you say?"

"Every word. All quotes on tape. All scenes verified in photos. You're safe as you were in your Mommy's tummy, chief. Now shut up and let me get back to becoming famous."

Vincenzo had to make certain of a few other editor-type details, like when I would be sending the photos, what restrictions I had agreed to, whether or not I felt he should be sending me more release forms, et cetera. Once he had gone over everything, however, for some reason my Brooklyn-born turtle was in no hurry to return me to the drudgery of making him look good. Taking a rare moment to slip into an almost human persona, he said:

"This is solid stuff, Carl. Good reporting. Good work. I mean it." Somewhat overwhelmed, I reminded him that it was Morgan Slate that had made the decision to put me in the right place at the right time. I was just doing my job. His normal growl roared back, reassuring me that it was really him on the other end as he shouted:

"I'm trying to pay you a compliment here, for Christ's sake, Carl. Did Slate write this copy? Did he make me see every inch of that farm house? No. Jesus, Mary and Joseph, Carl, I could almost smell that deputy's breakfast steaming. Couple more of these and we're going to put the **Dispatch** on the map."

"Wait until you see my piece of the barn."

"What happened in the barn?"

I gave him a preview, describing the wholesale slaughter of the Holister's livestock. I didn't have to give him much before he could see my angle. After reading of the horror in the house, then the next day we reveal what went on in the barn. While most news groups would just be assembling, we'd be ahead of the world. Twice over. I could feel the heat from Vincenzo's smile all the way across the country. He jabbered for another few moments over what great work I was doing, then finally asked the question I had been afraid to ask myself.

"Carl, this isn't going to turn into one of your 'monster of the week' pieces, is it?"

"Tony," I said slowly, trying not to launch us into an argument immediately, "I really want to say no, but ..."

"But what, Carl?"

"I don't know. I mean, if it is a man, what kind of man is capable of this kind of mayhem? The guy killed a lot of people in one night—tore apart a pack of dogs, rammed a shotgun through a person and pinned them to the wall with it. That might be explained simply enough by saying they're crazy. But ..."

"There's that word again."

"Yes," I half-growled, getting a tad annoyed, "there it is. And where it was leading was the barn. It's one thing to kill a family with your bare hands. But then thirty head of cattle? Two score hogs, a half dozen horses? You ever stand next to a horse, Tony?

What do you think it would take to knock one down, to tear its heart out of its chest, to break its neck and then rip its head off?"

The phone was silent. Hoping to make my point while the disturbing quiet continued, I said:

"All I'm saying is, what kind of crazy is strong enough to keep going that long? Seven people, a dozen dogs, then all that livestock ... that's a lot of killing. A lot of hard work. Cows are big, Tony. So are hogs. And this guy, not only does he kill and kill and kill, but he never slips up while doing any of it."

"What do you mean?"

"I mean I've got the coroner's word on it; once again, no evidence. All that blood, and so far not so much as a single fingerprint. More—not anything that could even be identified as a hand print. Or a footprint. Tony, some of these rooms were filled with blood, the carpets soaked with it. The coroner and I left tracks, and we were walking gingerly, trying to be as circumspect as possible. How does a guy crazed on a murder spree stay calm enough to tip toe around every pool of blood? How does he manage to not touch a single thing?"

Vincenzo's pause lasted so long it was almost frightening. I could hear him breathing, so I knew my answer hadn't killed him. But, I did find myself wondering if it had rendered him unconscious until finally he said:

"I'll be honest; I don't know how to answer you. But I'll say this, you remember Manson, Manson and his little family, going in and slaughtering a houseful of the rich and famous. No one could imagine such a thing then. It was the crime of the century." My turtle took himself another slight pause, then added:

"And that's what we've got here, Carl. It's the crime of the century. It's going to grab people by the ass and keep them glued to us until we provide them an answer. It's going to lock doors and shutter windows. If it moves out of that area, it's going to get people screaming for new legislation that allows them to buy guns and protect themselves with them."

"What're you talking about, Vincenzo," I said with obvious sarcasm. "We citizens are allowed to bear arms. It says so in the constitution. I remember my teacher telling me so."

"Constitution, constitution ..." Vincenzo said the word with a question in his voice, as if he knew he could remember what it meant if he just said it over enough times. After just a couple more tries, I heard the snapping of his pudgy fingers as he exclaimed,

"Oh, yeah, I remember, that's what they call toilet paper in the Senate—right?" Laughing, I told him:

"There could be a grain of truth in that."

We chuckled together for a few more seconds, then my buddy of a fleeting moment returned to being my never-ending editor. Business sliding back into his voice, he said:

"Listen, just stick to the facts, okay? Do up this barn piece, then get out there and start looking for more. And unless you have an actual picture of a dinosaur to run on page one, don't start calling the murderer 'it,' all right? Keep it 'he.' Is that too much to ask?"

I assured him it wasn't, then reminded him he was wasting time I could be using to keep us ahead of the competition. He hung up without saying another word. I wasn't angry with him for anything he had said. He hadn't said anything I hadn't been thinking myself. Yes, it was certainly obvious that something more than just routine murder was going on around here. That had been glaringly apparent since the first murder.

But, my little ten word message, coupled with the nightmare we found at the Holister spread, made it more than reasonable to cut loose the reins and let all the imaginations in the stable run wild. Still, Vincenzo had one thing right. I wasn't going to get anywhere if I stopped acting like a newsman. Not that I needed him to tell me that, but I wasn't going to argue the point. I had too much to do.

Simply being lucky enough to nail the story of the day was not going to be enough to keep me on top of what was happening in Gore for long. I was going to have to get out on the road and start looking into the whole picture. Wiffalon had given me a lot of details on what had happened in town behind the Gore Center Village, but he couldn't help me with Wendel Halford and what was to be found at the Happy Holland plant.

Because that was in another state. In someone else's jurisdiction. And if I wanted to know anything about what went on there, outside what I could read in the papers, then I was going to have to go there.

It was late in the afternoon, but on an impulse I grabbed up my company cell phone and punched in the number Wiffalon had given me for his opposite number in Two Hollows. After only a single ring a pleasant woman's voice identified the office she represented and asked me my business. I identified myself and asked if her boss could spare me a few minutes. She said she thought he might in a voice that was filled with a hint. Taking it, I told her I would be happy to wait while she checked.

In seconds I was patched through to Jedediah Peterson, the coroner for Two Hollows, West Virginia. He declared he was always happy to speak to the press, and that if I cared to drop in he would make time for me. Then, before I could suggest it, he asked if I'd like to meet him at Happy Holland's frozen yogurt plant. I told him that was a splendid idea, and that he had but to name the time. He told me:

"The days are getting shorter, you know. Probably you should jump in your car now and start headin' over. Call me when you see a big yellow sign for the plant. You'll know which one. I'll know you're close and I'll leave then."

"Thank you, sir," I told him. "I appreciate the courtesy."

"Don't think anything of it," he answered. "Just spell my name right in your paper."

As he hung up I smiled. Suddenly his wonderful cooperation was easily understandable. He was a publicity hound. That was fine by me. Guys like that always made things so much easier. Slipping on my new coat and grabbing up all my trade tools, I headed for the car. When I hit the parking lot, the sun's position gave me confidence we still had a solid two and half hours of daylight left.

Grateful, I jumped behind the wheel of my rental and revved its tiny, but willing engine to life. I checked my directions once more, then tore out of the parking lot, not so much breaking the speed limit as demolishing it. Normally I'm a fairly careful driver, but I wanted whatever Peterson had to offer. Tomorrow, when the news hordes started to arrive, he might decide information from him should come at a higher price.

Besides, I wasn't worried that day about a little speeding. After all, I told myself, it seemed all too likely that Will Jeeter and his boys were going to be a little too busy to be giving out speeding tickets that day. ●

CHAPTER TWELVE

I reached Two Hollows in record time. Peterson met me at the yogurt plant, already smoothing the way with the owners for him to give me a tour of the loading dock area. The day manager insisted on coming along. Since such couldn't have been better for me, I was inclined to attempt a cartwheel to express my joy at how things kept going my way. Knowing my turtle would prefer I practice some restraint, I merely said;

"That would actually be quite convenient, Mr. ...?"

"Jenks," he answered. "Ralph Jenks."

The three of us headed for the back of the plant at quite a rapid clip. Jenks was a short, wire brush of a man, compact, fast-moving. He kept his hair short, his shoes shined, and his tie rigidly clipped in place with a Happy Holland tie clip, basically just a standard gold clip with a windmill in the center, bordered on both sides by a set of wooden shoes.

If Jenks had no real outstanding characteristics, Peterson was nearly a perfect cipher. He was one of those people you simply didn't look twice at, or once for that matter. The man was overwhelmingly average. Height, weight, hair color, size of his ears, how straight he stood— everything about him had conspired since birth to make him the most unnoticeable human male on the face of the planet. And, sadly, it seemed he knew it.

It made it instantly obvious to me why he was shaping up as a publicity hound. Who could blame him? The most average looking guy on the planet, holding down a job where the majority of the people he dealt with were dead. If there was anyone who might want their picture in the paper it was him, a fact I filed away like any good reporter. I would bleed Mr. Peterson of all the information I could, tossing in whatever I could siphon off from Mr. Jenks along with it.

We exited through the back door, coming out onto the loading dock as Wendel would have had to come. As we did, Peterson asked:

"Shall I take you to the chalk outline?"

"Really," I said, a bit taken aback. "You actually drew a chalk outline?"

Jenks' head went back and forth from Peterson to myself and back again. The reason for his confusion was understandable. The day-shift man knew, of course, that there was no chalk outline. What he didn't know was how I knew. When he asked, the coroner told him:

"Because, Ralph, chalk outlines is just movie stuff. Nobody actually draws lines around dead bodies." Jenks actually looked a bit disappointed. As he turned his head to me, his expression hoping I could repudiate this shocking news, I was forced to back up Peterson.

"It's true," I said. "Chalk outlines have been used to mark the place of crime victims, especially shooting victims, so they could be moved for treatment. So they can get them off to the hospital while leaving the cops a reasonable idea of how they landed."

"Oh, I get it," said the day man. "Then the cops can keep looking at the crime scene without making some dying guy stick around and bleed to death."

"By George, he's got it."

"I'll tell you a funny story," I offered as we walked down the stairs from the loading dock and out onto the pavement. "This comes out of Baltimore, and the cops there swear it's a true story. Shooting victim is on the ground—unconscious. Cop's drawing a chalk outline around him so he can be moved when the paramedics get there. Well, the guy wakes up while the cop is still drawing the line. He sees this, and says, 'Oh my God, I'm dead.' Then, he slumps back down, and just dies."

The coroner and Jenks both stared at me for a second. I could tell that Peterson was questioning whether I was kidding or not. The day manager was simply trying to gauge whether or not it was appropriate to laugh. I merely shrugged, told them again that the cops I know in Baltimore swear it's the truth, and then suggested we get on with our tour. Peterson agreed. Jenks turned his head to hide his grin.

Debate over the veracity of Baltimore's finest ended only seconds later as we came to the spot where the majority of Wendel Halford's remains had been discovered. All in all, it was a quite easy spot to find.

"We didn't do any clean-up yet," Jenks mentioned, "because Mr. Peterson here asked us not to."

"True," the coroner added. "Even though I had signed off on the case, I asked the area remain undisturbed for a few days, give me time to see if I thought of something else we might be able to try." Pointing back toward the loading dock, he said:

"As you can see, the trucks that need to use this area can do so and avoid this section with only a bit of maneuvering."

"But," I asked, "I thought Halford had been killed right at the back door. Obviously from all the blood he did so over here, but..."

"Wire service man got it wrong," explained Peterson. Walking back and forth, his hands and arms suddenly becoming far more animated, the coroner lectured:

"Wendel was snatched over by the door. I found the butt there from the cigarette he'd been smoking—his prints, his saliva—along with skid marks from the heel of his left shoe. But who or whatever got him grabbed him by the door and dragged him over here. If you get down and really look, you'll find the same skid marks scattered across the way from there to here."

I nodded my head while snapping pictures, letting Peterson lecture me as if I'd never stepped beyond a stream of yellow police tape before. The more he was allowed to pontificate, the greater chance there was he'd either let slip with something really juicy, something he wasn't supposed to allow anyone outside his office to know about, or that I might spot something on my own.

Not that there was all that much to see. Halford had been torn into bloody bits. All the bits had long been taken away, leaving only the blood for us to amuse ourselves with. I took a string of shots from different angles, giving Vincenzo as many different ways to show the site as possible. I also got Peterson to pose there in the open lot, and then Jenks. Tight-lipped as the day man was, it was possible he might still say something quotable, and I wanted the **Dispatch** to have the glossy to go with it.

"We can tell that who or whatever killed Halford was exceedingly tall."

"How so?"

"Blood dripping from the killer's hands," he answered. "When it hits the ground, the radius of its bounce lets us determine from how high it came. Now, really that tells us how high the killer can reach. You see ..."

Peterson extended his arm, holding his hand straight up over his head. He then moved his hand up and down, explaining that the blood rings he measured could have been created from any height, but that doing so at least told them an approximation of the killer's arm length and height. The coroner admitted it was possible they might be dealing with a short freak with incredibly long arms but, as he put it:

"Anything's possible, in this best of all possible worlds—sure. But my job calls for playing the averages. Besides, this guy is freaky enough." My reporter's alarm bell went off instantly, warning me that I had a big fish on my line, but that it had to be played carefully. Putting my hand over my mouth to cover a make-believe yawn, I feigned disinterest as I asked:

"Freaky? What's that mean?"

My eyes were closed, part of my fake yawn. Peterson wanted attention; I'd been able to smell that since our first words to each other on the phone. If he could see my eyes, he'd know just how interested I was in hearing what he had to say. And, seeing that interest might remind him just what he was supposed to be talking about and what he was supposed to keep within his department.

I had to remember that he was fishing as well. For his type, seeing that desire for an exclusive fact, for that fatal slip, could be just enough to turn off the spigot. But I needed him talking, so I stretched my performance a couple of extra seconds, mumbling an apology. Then, as if I had already forgotten my question, I began to shut down my camera, hoping it looked to Jenks and Peterson that all my attention was focused on that.

It was enough.

"Freaky," I could feel the line going tight in my hands. "I'll tell you about freaky. This guy, from the best guess we can make, and you gotta know, we had the state team in here, even assuming that his arms are exceedingly long—fingertips down to, or below the knee—has got to be at least eight feet tall."

"Eight feet," I repeated, still pretending to be concentrating on my camera. "Huh. That should make him easy to spot."

"You'd think," snorted Jenks.

"Eight feet, at least," Peterson repeated. "At **least**."

I nodded thoughtfully, pursing my lips as if I'd suddenly been given a great deal to think about. Both men talked for a bit longer, but there were no other exciting tidbits to be gathered. I listened politely, just on the off chance something else might turn up. One never knows.

While I did, however, something about the site of Wendel Halford's execution kept nagging at me. I stared at it, wondering what the back of my mind was trying to get me to notice. Casually, I walked around the area, head downward, eyes focused on the ten to fifteen square feet where the thickest coating of blood was to be found, but nothing focused my attention.

I knew some part of me had noticed something, that some vague memory was attempting to assert itself, but I couldn't put that specific two together with any other twos at that moment. For the life of me, all I could see was a stretch of pavement, all of it just like every other bit of it there in the loading dock. Except, of course, that that particular stretch of it was covered in blood. Elsewise, it was just another patch of moss-encrusted concrete, sitting next to a lawn, leading to a very high fence which cut the forest beyond off from the Happy Holland property line.

A forest in which no one could find any tracks leading toward it or away from it. A fence that showed no marks of anyone climbing up or down it. Peterson confirmed that—no pressure bends, no hair or bits of clothing caught in the razor wire running across its top. I made certain of that by asking him again just before we left. He told me:

"Nope, and that's the puzzler. We can rule out those few people working at the plant that night. No blood inside the plant, on the loading dock—nothing. They were all inside when Halford was found, and there was no way the killer could have cleaned up out here and gone back in."

Peterson folded his hands over his chest, and then turned to stare at the fence. Looking it up and down once more, hoping to find an answer he could share with the reporter from the big city who could make him a celebrity for a handful of seconds if he could but just be brilliant, he said absently:

"Nope, it's a locked room mystery. The gate was locked, so the killer had to come over the fence. The plant was locked from the inside, so he had to go back out the same way. But, except for a few leaves, we didn't find a blessed thing stuck up there." He shook his head sadly, the slump of his shoulders letting me know he was accepting defeat as he said again:

"Not a blessed thing."

The three of us headed back for the loading dock at that point. I congratulated myself on picking up a prize bit of information, chuckling slyly over the fact I had it on tape. Indeed, I entered the yogurt plant quite pleased with myself, forgetting that there really are none so blind as those who will not see. ●

CHAPTER THIRTEEN

After promising Peterson that I would be certain to spell his name correctly, I headed for my second stop there in Two Hollows. I left the local police for last. The one good thing about cops almost everywhere is they don't shut down for the evening and go home, opening back up for business in the morning. But, private citizens pretty much do, and they don't usually take kindly to people rapping on their doors once the sun goes down, especially by reporters. Take it from one who knows.

And thus, armed with directions I was able to get from a combination of Jenks and two of his people at the plant, I arrived at the home of the late Wendel Halford roughly twenty minutes before sundown. Close enough, I told myself, heading for the front door. I left my rental car in the street next to the yard; there was no sidewalk. As I headed up the walk, I noted Wendel's truck in the driveway. I knew it was his because its somewhat bizarre purple color was one of the landmarks Jenks' fellows had told me would mark his house for certain.

They had also mention Mrs. Halford's white Honda, but had said nothing about a Lexus. That meant the widow had company—company that could afford luxury cars. It might have been her insurance man; considering its dark color, it might have been the local funeral director. Then again, the back of my mind growled at me, it could also be her rich uncle, the local banker or any of a hundred other guesses. The only way I was going to find out was to ring the bell and weasel my way inside. Straightening my tie, I rang the bell, then hurriedly ran my fingers through my hair and slapped my hat back on as the door opened.

"Yes ..."

A not bad looking woman in her mid-thirties answered the door.

She matched the description of Veronica Halford I'd been given—blonde hair, shoulder length, brown eyes, oval face, nice figure—or, as the boys at Happy Holland had put it, "a full behind and a great rack." They were an earthy pair, but essentially correct. The widow Halford also did not seem as if she was going to be wearing black for long.

"Good evening, Mrs. Halford?"

"Yes, I'm Veronica Halford. May I help you?"

"You could, ma'am. My name is Carl Kolchak; I'm a reporter with the *Hollywood Dispatch*. I was wondering if you could spare me a few moments of your time?"

"Certainly; come on in."

She granted me entrance as if I were the paperboy collecting for the week. Whatever adjectives I unleashed upon the page to describe the widow to the world, I was thinking "bereaved" would probably not be one of them. She seemed a touch on edge, the kind of edge most people go to great lengths to hide. As I wondered why she even let me inside, I caught a whiff of her breath as she turned. Bourbon has a wonderful way of making people careless.

The widow gestured toward an oversized chair, then proceeded to the couch directly across the coffee table from it. I thanked her and, after shrugging off my overcoat which I threw over the chair's back, settled in to see what I might accomplish. I noted that there were two glasses next to the bottle on the table, confirming my notion that the Lexus did not make its permanent home in the Halford driveway. As I wondered where its owner was, however, Mrs. Halford returned to her drink, telling me:

"I kinda figured once they found that other body torn apart over in Gore that your kind was going to start crawling out of the woodwork. So, you know what I did?"

"No ma'am, not really."

"I told myself that whichever one of you showed up first, I would answer all their questions. Then tell the rest of them to go talk to the first guy. I've got things to do, you know."

"I understand completely. I take it I must be the first person from the media to visit since those who came to talk to you at the time of your husband's death?"

"Yeah. And there weren't that many of them. Just local boys. Did you really say you came here all the way from Hollywood?" When I let her know her hearing had not failed her, she looked through me to some moment in her past and confided in me:

"You know, I almost went to California, try to break into the movies. I used to be something to look at. I'm serious."

"Yes, ma'am."

"I was. I was hot stuff. You don't think I was hot stuff?"

My mind raced for the proper response. Usually one is not called upon to comment on the relative "wow" level of widows, even one that had been drinking, possibly since the funeral. Veronica's speech was beginning to slur just a trifle around the edges, giving me the problem members of my community have when interviewing the tipsy. Getting an elected official to say something off the record while in their cups is considered a moral victory in my circles. Stumbling across some embarrassing tidbit in the spew from a grieving drunk was thought of as two rungs down the ladder from tacky.

Before I could sink any further into discomfort, however, a noise known to every person civilized enough to enjoy the wonders of indoor plumbing revealed to me where the owner of the Lexus I'd noted outside had been keeping themselves. Somehow the sound caught the attention of my hostess as well, and I could see the desire to have her question answered melt from her eyes.

In seconds, a handsome, well-dressed man, also in his midthirties, entered the room. He was large, the way football players are large. He stopped suddenly as he stepped into the room, the look on his face letting me know he was surprised to find someone else there. For a moment I thought he seemed to recognize me, then decided it was probably just the curse of my new overcoat, which I was beginning to think should have an albatross embroidered on its breast where the polo shirt people usually stick their alligators.

"Hello..." he said, offering his hand. "Mark Kenny. And you are...?"

I took the man's hand, introducing myself as I shook it. I then said it seemed as if I had arrived at a terrible time, and that perhaps I should come back at one that was a bit more suitable. Veronica protested immediately, telling Kenny she wanted to talk to the reporter from Hollywood. His attitude was much like hers, albeit a trifle more sober—now that there had been a second murder, more reporters were inevitable. Grabbing up his drink, he began to retreat to the far end of the couch, then said:

"Excuse me, Mr. Kolchak, where are our manners? Can we get

you anything? Hard or soft? Coffee, even? Water?"

I begged off, explaining that while I appreciated the hospitality, I had a very tight schedule to keep. I also hinted that I was feeling badly at having arrived at such an inopportune moment, as if such made me uncomfortable. To sound believable I simply did my best impersonation of Updyke. They seemed to buy it.

Getting down to the facts, I did my best to get Veronica on the record in all the normal ways—how was she holding up; what did she think happened; did she miss Wendel; was she provided for—blah, blah, blah. It was as great a load of nonsense as such drivel always is, but it's part of the job. It's also good cover for trying to get at what a reporter is always really after.

As Veronica talked for the tape recorder, and Mark sat in the corner nursing his drink, I paid as much attention to what she had to say as I did to the random traffic noises outside. I didn't care if Veronica Halford missed her Wendel. When you come right down to it, nobody cares about such nonsense.

There's an old adage in the news business that goes: no one cares about the death of millions as much as they do their dog getting hit by a bus. It's true. People vulture over the evening news looking for folks with worse lives to make themselves feel better about the crap they have to wade through every day. No, I could care less about Veronica and Wendel.

But Veronica and Mark had me very interested.

What I became fascinated by there in the crackerbox-sized living room where Wendel had watched his football games and set up the Christmas tree every year, et cetera, was watching Mark Kenny sweat. He was massively concerned about something, but what that something was I wasn't certain. Could he actually be that upset over being caught with the widow? Some people can be made to blush easily, but Kenny didn't give me the impression of being one of them. Deciding there might be something in rattling his chain, I asked in my most innocent voice:

"So, tell me, Mr. Kenny, how did you feel about Wendel's death?"

The man who drove a black Lexus rather than a purple truck looked as if I'd just hit him between the eyes with a sack of wet socks. As he sputtered, Veronica attempted to come to his rescue by offering:

"Oh, Mark here didn't know Wendel, ah, not all that well, I mean."

"Oh, no...?"

"Veronica and I met at Haberton," offered Kenny finally. "Oh, ah yes, you're not from around here. Haberton is the local college. I'm a... a professor there. Veronica was in one of my classes. We've become friends over the last few months, you know how it is, now with this, this tragedy—"

I stopped him there, pretending that I hadn't heard anything in his voice except his words. He calmed somewhat, enough anyway to drain his drink and begin to build another. As I made polite noises and asked several more pointless questions, my mind whirled around the question of Mark Kenny.

Although I had no idea what it might be at that moment, there was definitely something up with the widow's gentleman caller. He was far too nervous, too agitated, to simply be embarrassed. Yes, he was acting guilty as the cat spitting yellow feathers, but if I didn't know better, I would have almost thought he was acting guilty about more than just appearances.

Yes—I'll admit it, I've been around werewolves and witches and other normal types who turn into other things at a moment's notice. If it were a movie, or worse, some cheap TV show, I could well have thought Mark Kenny turned into a horrible beast at certain preordained moments and went forth on slaughtering rampages. But, **because** I've been around so much of the strange and the terrifying, I was certain Kenny was not the murderer the entire country would soon be obsessing over. He didn't give off that feel. The vibration spilling off him was confusing, but I knew whatever he was hiding, it wasn't the fact that he was the silent killer of the Virginias.

Also, at that point I knew I'd gotten all I was going to get there sitting in Wendel Halford's chair. A policeman could have asked different questions, having the power to force some answers. If I was to try something like that, all that would happen would be the righteous widow would end up calling a policeman. No, a reporter has to know when to cut bait and when to pull in their line to wait for another day.

Besides, I told myself, not only did I not want to scare my little fishies there in the Halford pond until I had something more to go on, but I had a hot date that night. Thanking the pair of them for all their time and trouble, acting as if I wouldn't have noticed if they had mounted each other there in front of me, I gathered up my tape recorder, dutifully got Mrs. Halford to pose for a picture, and then packed all my paraphernalia away in my bag. Thanking Veronica once more at the door for all her help, I made the obligatory noises of consolement, then added:

"Oh, and ma'am, to answer your question of before, not to be forward during your time of mourning, but I think Hollywood missed out when you decided to stay here."

I shook her hand and gave her a tiny bow, my eyes on Kenny the entire time. He rewarded my efforts by glaring intently, letting me know that, at the very least, there was no reason not to assume that he and Veronica were lovers, and that they had not waited until after the funeral to become so.

What that information was going to mean to my story would depend on what I could find out about one Mark Kenny after I made a trip out to the ivy-covered halls of Haberton College. I don't know what I expected to find there—one never does at that stage of the game—but I was willing to bet every dollar left in my *Dispatch* expense account that I was going to uncover something interesting.

If I'd had the slightest idea how interesting, I might not have been so glib about the whole thing. ●

CHAPTER FOURTEEN

The drive back from Two Hollows was achieved in record time. I was able to hit the motel, bang out two thousand words for my desperately waiting turtle, email it off and then change into a fresh shirt all within the margin of safety I had set for myself earlier. I made it to The Green Circle, the restaurant LuAnn had pointed out that morning, ten minutes before we were supposed to meet, twenty minutes before she arrived.

"Well, hello," I said, rising to take her coat.

Her fashionably late entrance was one worth waiting for. She had broken out both her high heels and the good pearls—both of which told me volumes. She'd been in sensible shoes that morning. That meant she only donned her hunting gear when she had her bomb sites set on something. And where it was true the pearls could have been fakes, they had enough of that deep, milky luster that let me know I was being lured—especially considering the neckline within which they had been suspended.

"Waiting long?"

"For you," I asked, unable to keep a smile from dominating my face, "pretty much all my life. But you're here now, so why make a big deal out of it? Me? I'd rather make up for lost time."

She smiled back, her eyes giving me enough appreciation to let me know I'd passed the test. A waitress came as soon as I'd finished helping LuAnn with her coat and her chair. Not feeling any need to rush, we ordered from the bar. My date surprised me slightly by asking for a Scotch on the rocks with a twist. I'd been in some sort of condescending mood, I suppose, expecting her to order some overly sweet girlie drink—something smelling of coconut and too many spoonfuls of sugar. I had my Scotch like I always do, warm and unadorned.

I was advised to find something from the wonderful world of pork products. LuAnn's advise was quite sensibly thought out. First off, she said, the Appalachians were not the place to look for quality seafood. No one could really mess up beef, but pigs were the local cash crop, and everyone for a hundred miles in every direction had at least one perfect recipe for turning pork into ambrosia. As for chicken, she intimated that any of the fowl there was fine enough, but that I might need something with a bit more "staying power." Deciding things had been going my way enough that I could assume I knew what she meant, I ordered the stuffed porkchops.

Dinner was, for an evening in the life of this reporter, anyway, a thing most welcome. The salad was fresh enough; the soup not from a can. The porkchops were three fingers-thick, filled with a wonderful sausage and raisin stuffing, all of it drenched in the same mushroom onion gravy that had been used to turn the mashed potatoes into something you could picture the merest memory of keeping a starving man going just one more day.

The side dish that came with the meal was applesauce doused in cinnamon, and whoever had put that trio together on the menu earned their year-end bonus six times over in my book. The applesauce came in a chilled bowl, keeping it frosty cold so that you could dunk your steaming meat in it and then plop the whole onion/apple, hot/cold confection in your mouth. It was an American answer to China's sweet & sour dishes, and it made me more than happy–it made me content. Almost as content as I was over the fact I was sitting there in the Green Circle, looking across the table and having LuAnn Hildebergen to talk to, to look at.

To be with.

"Mr. Kolchak," she said with mock demureness, "I swear you're enough to make a girl blush. Wherever did you learn to stare at a woman so?"

"Oh, I picked that up from my dad," I told her. Purposely keeping my eyes on her, doing my best to see the thoughts within her head, I said, "he would stare at my mother all the time. Big bug eyes following her around the house. Oh, yes—sometimes he wouldn't go to work for weeks at a time. What did he say it was, now let me see ... something about the shape of ..."

"You don't say?"

"Oh no," I swore, using a voice that hinted I might be exaggerating, just the slightest. "It's true; I swear. He really couldn't take his eyes off her."

"Ummm-hummmm ..."

"Did I tell you I have twenty-three brothers and sisters?"

That was the line that did it. LuAnn nearly did a classic sitcom spit-take. She managed to avoid low comedy, for which I was grateful since her aim might have been disastrous considering our proximity, but she began giggling then which on her was wonderfully attractive. For some women laughter is a deadly enemy, revealing them to be obnoxious, foolish creatures. Not LuAnn.

Captured by the moment, she seemed more charming than ever, delightful in her sudden vulnerability. Her chuckle fit lasted for only a handful of seconds, but it had been enough. Playtime between us was over. Whatever decision she was going to make about us had been made. Regaining her composure, she said to me:

"Twenty-three brothers and sisters, hummmm?" When I nodded, she asked, "And do they all have as much of the devil in them as you do?"

"Oh, no," I told her, my face as straight as I could maintain it. "Of course, I can't really swear there were twenty-four of us al together—"

"Oh, why is that?"

"Well, a lot of the others were kept in the attic, a few in the basement. We never really saw them."

"Not even at mealtime?"

"No. My sister Leroy would take a bucket of fish heads up to the attic... I can't remember who fed the kids in the basement."

"That so...?"

"Oh, yes. You see ..."

I was prepared to say more, but LuAnn stretched her arm across the table and placed two of her fingers against my lips. She did not speak as she did so, just left that nicely toned length of smooth arm extended from her to me. I didn't speak, either. But I fixed my eyes on hers, and I kissed her fingers, softly, but with a pressure that let her know I wasn't going to stop until she stole her hand away from me.

As the color rose in her cheeks, and the fire in her eyes, I did my best to signal for the check as nonchalantly as possible.

In a way I was actually embarrassed taking LuAnn back to the Motel 1,2,3!. Suddenly, no matter what picture of me she had put together within her mind, I knew it had to be shattered by the reality of my place in the food chain as made obvious by such lodgings. To her undying credit, she did not seem to notice. I allowed her superior acting ability to perform its task of not ruining our evening.

We made good use of the room, testing the sturdiness of several of its furnishings. I am happy to report that Motel 1,2,3!'s furnishings survived their workout. Further inspection of our accommodations proved that their showers were deceptively large, capable of holding two people at the same time after all.

When we finally returned to bed, weary but clean, we spent a little time curled around one another, simply holding on, grateful for the feeling that someone still wanted to touch us. Maybe I shouldn't speak for her, but I thought I sensed that same need I was feeding by touching her, being near her.

It's a mood most don't want to talk about, embarrassed to even admit to themselves that desperate want grinding away in the center of their gut. We only managed to be comfortable with ourselves for some twenty minutes before we had to start chattering. She asked me about my work. I told her about my busy morning. She was understandably interested.

Since the first two articles I'd shipped to Vincenzo would be hitting the street soon enough—one that night, the second in the morning—I told her much of what had happened. The thought of such goings on made her shudder openly. She moved against me unconsciously. I might not be anyone's idea of an All American Hero—even my own—but I was nearby and I was warm, and that was enough to provide the comfort she needed from the reality that a murderer was on the loose whose motivations could not be predicted or even understood.

To help her relax, I asked her about her work. She filled me in on the exciting days spent by most research assistants, letting me know how exceedingly dull her own professor's needs had proven to be. Mention of her boss rang a small bell in the back of my mind. Trying to be casual, I asked:

"By the way, you wouldn't happen to know a professor by the name of Mark Kenny, would you?"

I felt a slight stiffness run through her. It was an involuntary thing, something she couldn't avoid because of the unexpectedness of the question. For a moment I thought she was going to pretend not to know Kenny, but instead she said:

"How do you know Professor Kenny?"

She said his title as if it were spelled with only four letters. I told her about running into him at the Halford home. I played it as innocently as I could, wanting to see what she would offer me about him. She had more than a little to say.

"Can I say that we're not the best of friends and let it go at that?"

"You could ..."

"Oh, please don't get upset about Mark Kenny. He's just a grabby type, thinks he owns all the women who walk the halls. Would never dream of touching a student, of course—he's not a complete idiot ..."

I reserved the right to comment on that thought later, simply listening for the moment instead.

"I've had a few run-ins with him. When polite words, then not so polite words didn't work, I finally ended up stomping on his foot. He had his hands caught in the folds of my skirt at the time, so he really couldn't say anything about it."

I made noises that were supposed to comfort her; she tried to get back in the mood. It didn't work. Wherever the two of us might have been headed that evening, I had pitched that particular destination out the window by bringing up Kenny. We made a half-hearted stab at intimacy afterward, but the magic was gone, knocked to the ground and swept under the rug by the memory of Mark Kenny's roving hands.

LuAnn made a show of dressing for me. Some women can make the simple act of putting on clothing look like a strip-tease in reverse. Really, she barely did anything more than move slowly, but if she had smiled at the end and jumped back into bed, I found I was ready to welcome her. She didn't, however, and I kept my lower half safely hidden from sight under the blanket.

She came to my side and kissed my cheek, a soulful smile letting me know she understood why her gentleman was not escorting her to the door. We assured each other that dinner again the next evening was a done deal, and after we made certain we each had the other's number, she went to the door and disappeared out into the parking lot.

I stared at the door for a long while, replaying the after-image of her over and over in my mind. Finally the back of my brain got tired of all the repetition and insisted I find something else to do.

A glance at the laptop reminded me that I could always get an article ahead, or transcribe some of my tapes from the day. A glance at my luggage reminded me I was not yet out of liquor.

I leave it to you to guess how dedicated to the glory of the *Hollywood Dispatch* I remained, there in my Motel 1,2,3! suite, alone and cold. To quote the bogus Santa Claus Edmund Gwynn almost thrashes at the beginning of "Miracle on 34th Street;"

A man's got to do something to keep warm. ●

CHAPTER FIFTEEN

The next morning found me barely conscious as Mel banged on my door at 7:00 A.M., 1,2,3!'s answer to a wake-up call. I told him there was five bucks in it for him if he came back in a half hour with a pair of large black coffees and resumed his banging again—ten bucks if he made it an hour. He returned at 8:30 and I thought about making it fifteen, but gave him the ten I said I would. As I staggered my wounded self back to sit on my bed with my bag of coffees, he asked:

"Not that I mind, but why did you leave a wake-up call for seven if you didn't want to get up at seven?"

"Good intentions," I mumbled. He accepted the answer and headed back for his office to await his next chance to perform for the greater glory of 1,2,3!.

Using the coffee to lubricate my throat, I began swallowing pain killers one after another. I keep a small bottle with an assortment of over-the-counter and left-over prescription odds and ends mixed together for those hard-to-rise mornings. Now, please understand that just drinking isn't enough to wear me down that bad. No, the town of Gore had conspired to put me through a rough night. Of course, a big part of my bad night was the back of my mind irrationally punishing me for messing up with LuAnn. Not that I could have known about her personal antipathy toward Kenny, but that's kind of what the word "irrational" means.

The rest of my tossing and turning could be blamed upon the sights and smells found at the Holister place, feeling sorry for poor Wendel Halford after meeting the widow Halford, and some slight paranoia over everyone staring at me simply because I'd bought the wrong overcoat. Staggering to the bathroom mirror, I took a good look at my face, wondering if I'd see the old me there when I could finally focus.

After several splashes of cold water, sure enough, there was the old Carl Kolchak, staring dumbly at me as if he had any right replacing that wonderful fellow who'd been looking sharp and feeling confident in there yesterday. The stranger was gone, replaced by the fellow I was used to seeing, him of the haggard expression—bewildered, tired, beaten down—useless.

Yesterday I'd looked in the same sheet of glass and found someone Vincenzo and Slate could reasonably be proud of, a crackerjack reporter who swept into town and latched onto the story of the century. The guy I saw there today, he was the idiot who kept shouting "vampire" in crowded rooms—the boob who seemed to spend his every waking hour looking to get me into some kind of trouble. Finding him back in my life so quickly did not help my recovery any.

Waiting for the pills to start hammering me into some kind of shape where I could face the world, I sat at 1,2,3!'s idea of a desk and finished transcribing my tapes from the day before. I didn't type out every word, just those quotes I knew I could use. After as many years as I'd put into the business, I knew the winners when I heard them.

In between my short bursts of keyboarding, I finished my coffee, shaved, and crawled into a clean set of clothes. Some judicious fast- forwarding got the entire process over and done with by 9:45. As reasonably ready for the day as I supposed I was going to get, I headed back to Larry's and let him feed me once more. The meal was as filling as the one I'd had up the street the night before, but it was nowhere near as enjoyable.

After breakfast I found myself feeling somewhat more normal. Paying the check, I asked Larry what medical school he attended, letting him know that was how much better I was doing with one of his meals in me. The left-over hippy chef said it was just the natural benefit of not buying into a corrupt system. I didn't argue; for all I knew he was right.

My second stop was to drop in on Sheriff Jeeter at his office. I was introduced to those other deputies who were in the building, as well as Mrs. Dorthina, a rail-thin black woman who answered the phones, took messages, did the filing, and any and all the other things anyone could think to ask of her. She was that one long-suffering woman one finds in any office, who keeps everything running without anyone noticing. Oh, I was certain there was a cake for her on every birthday, and that the sheriff and others gave lip service to the time-honored phrase, "we couldn't do it without you," but she had that look of neglect—by those around her at work, and the world in general.

"Carl," said Jeeter, his eyes looking half-glazed over already. "I put a call in to all the airports that feed this area. Would it surprise you to know that there isn't a rental car to be had at any of them?"

"Sorry about that, chief," I told him, quoting the late Don Adams. "You figuring the onslaught has begun?"

"Don't sweat it," he answered, obviously referring to the story I'd filed last night. "There's already a dozen of them out there—those what could drive here." He sighed quietly, then added, "Ahhh, hell, it's not like we could've kept the Holister place a secret. It's not Russia around here yet."

"Russia's not Russia anymore, sheriff," quipped one of the deputies. "Get with the times."

"I hate these kids," Jeeter announced with a wry smile. "And don't you want too much from me, Mr. Kolchak, or I'll start hatin' reporters, too." Holding my hands up in front of my chest, palms toward the sheriff, I shook them for comic effect, answering:

"No, no... although I was hoping to borrow one of your children here... old timer."

When Campbell grinned at my comment, Jeeter nailed him with a look, adding:

"Okay, wiseguy, you think he's so funny, you get to babysit. What'd you need?"

"I was hoping to get behind Gore Center Village today, check out the second crime scene. It's still off-limits, yes?"

"Yeah, but it shouldn't be, I suppose," Jeeter conceded. "Most of the owners over there have thrown at least one fit at me somewhere during the last twenty-four hours, wanting to use their back doors again. Awwhh, hell, yeah—Allen, run Carl over there, show him what we found, and while he takes his little pictures and dreams about gettin' back to the big city, go ahead and take down our tape and load up the barricades." The sheriff thought for a moment, then added:

"Better take your truck."

Campbell seemed grateful for duty that didn't involve the Holister spread. I understood his reluctance to return there. It's one thing to know you're heading into a bad scene, it's another to stumble across one, one that goes on room after room, and floor after floor.

We chatted pleasantly on the way to the second crime scene. He didn't ask any really tough questions and I didn't tell him any really big lies. Once behind the Gore Center Village, the deputy pointed out the spot that obviously had been the site where still-unknown victim number two was torn to shreds. I asked him to leave the yellow tape up while I took my pictures. He responded that he'd take a moment to go door to door and let the Village merchants know use of their alley would soon be returned to them.

There really wasn't much to see there. In many ways, the spot behind the Happy Holland loading dock was more dramatic, offered a better range of photo ops. Ultimately, though, they were essentially the same site. There was no doubt the same killer had been at work in both locations. Both were characterized by a monstrous, wild abandon in the way the victim's blood was splattered everywhere. Both were desolate, flat stretches of asphalt, dull and plain and ordinary, cracked and old and moss-encrusted. I stood above the long-dried blood, staring, searching it for something the experts might have missed.

I didn't know what I was looking for, of course. In truth, I had no real idea that there was actually anything to look for. I was simply staring, trying to justify my expense account. You have to realize, thanks to all those old films you can only find these days in rest homes like Turner Classic Movies, every reporter thinks that sooner or later he's going to solve: *the big case.*

This kind of nonsense gets into our brains thanks to screenwriters who are forever thinking that newsmen, as well as little old ladies, skateboarding teenagers, et cetera, are all more qualified to solve murders than the police. All the cops have is massive investigation squads, trained forensic experts, pathology teams, and so forth. While we, we the people, that is, we've got moxie.

And then, one small, chilling detail leaped out at me like a motivated urban youth going for a senior citizen's purse. For a moment I was speechless, driven to silence by an overwhelming paralysis brought about by suddenly making a horrible connection between crime scene one and crime scene two.

Quickly I walked from one end of the alley behind Gore Center Village to the other. Not finding anywhere that which I dreaded I would not find, I got down on my hands and knees and inspected the crime scene more closely. Afraid to touch anything, I screamed to Campbell, shouting for him to return. He was by my side in less than half a minute.

"What's wrong, Mr. Kolchak?"

"Deputy, I don't think you should take down the barriers just yet." When he protested that the sheriff had told him to, I asked him to contact Jeeter. In seconds I was on his hand-held with his boss. When he asked what I was up to, I told him:

"Listen, I think I've spotted something. Before I go out on a limb and say anything, however, I'd like to go back over to Happy Holland, and then out to the Holister place. I'd like to do this fast, too. Campbell running his cherry would certainly help."

There was a long pause. I'd helped prepare Jeeter for the wave of media that was already washing over his town. On the other hand, I was a civilian, and a Californian to boot. One with a bad reputation for harassing the police and claiming to have seen things beyond most people's comprehension. Finally, however, he had me put him back on the radio with Campbell. After what felt like an insanely long pause, the deputy holstered his radio, saying:

"Looks like I've been promoted to being a chauffeur to the stars. Where to first, swami?"

"Happy Holland Frozen Yogurt, over in Two Hollows. And don't spare the horsepower." ●

CHAPTER SIXTEEN

Campbell drove us straight to the back side of Happy Holland, threading his way through a line-up of eighteen wheelers all there presumably to pick up products to transport across the nation. He had asked me what the problem was when we first set out. As we both clambered into his truck, I'd answered him as best I could.

"Allen, did you ever pray you were wrong about something? Did you ever come up against a set of facts that made you want to disbelieve that two plus two could add up to anything—let alone four?"

As he slid his key into the ignition, I could see it in his eyes; maybe it was putting together the facts that let him know his girlfriend was cheating on him, or that a parent was going to die, that there was a reason his dog hadn't come home for three days—whatever. He understood.

"That's where I am right now." Feeling myself starting to shake, I told him, "For now, please—you just drive. Let me go back to praying–hell, make that begging."

He'd nodded, thrown his cherry on top of his truck, and off we had headed. I've actually been in more than one police car in my time when it was racing all out at top speed. It can really be exciting. That day was probably exciting, too, but I didn't notice. I was too busy, alternately praying that I really had lost my mind, and growling at Heaven in my head for cursing me so.

Why, I wanted to know? Why me? Just what had I done during my years in Vegas to deserve all this? I could have taken bribes in New York and stayed on top of the world. I could have nodded, looked the other way, and have become a well-positioned part of the machine that ran Chicago. But no, I had to do it the Carl Kolchak way, acting the role of a righteous fool who thought telling the truth got you somewhere.

It got me somewhere, all right. It got me banished to wandering in the desert, trying to recreate a career in the modern Sodom known as Las Vegas. And, after falling from the heights to land in that Hell, I found that what I thought was the bottom was really only the halfway point in my descent downward. Had I learned to play ball yet? No, of course not. Not me, not Carl Kolchak. Not God's gift to journalism.

No, I had to go right back to being the same miserable fool I'd been all along. Offered another chance to play with the big dogs, to share a secret with the powers that be, to prove I was a reliable sort who could be trusted, I had to immediately bite every hand offered, screaming to the heavens about a vampire. And then everything else. The endless parade of nightmares that have been visited upon me ever since.

"Why me, God?"

I muttered the words in a low, but angry voice. Campbell didn't pretend he thought I was talking to him, or make some feeble attempt to get me to "open up." Like I said, he looked into my eyes and knew what I was talking about. Indeed, all my comment spurred him to do was push down harder on the gas pedal.

By the time we tore into Happy Holland I really was shaking. The weight of what I was thinking had gotten to me and I found myself pushed into the corner of the truck's cab, almost on the verge of tears. Don't get me wrong; they weren't tears of fear, terror over what I thought I'd figured out. No, they were worse. It was self pity that had me trembling. It was terror over the thought that it was never going to end. That everywhere I went, there were always going to be monsters. There were always going to be bodies. There were always going to be oceans of innocent blood. And that I was always going to be laughed at, or threatened, or manhandled, simply for telling the truth about any of it.

"Mr. Kolchak..." Campbell's voice was quiet, but urgent. "We're here, sir."

Well, I thought, a cop treating me with respect. I guess that was something. Of course, it was the respect one shows a growling dog that fear has backed into a corner, or an escaped lunatic whose actions you simply cannot predict. It was so pathetic it made me laugh.

"Ahhhh... Mr. Kolchak...?"

I have no idea how long I sat there, tittering to myself, giggling like the madman I'd just spent the entire trip praying I was. Maybe I wanted to force God's hand, maybe it was the back of my brain's way of begging him to let this cup pass. Whichever, it didn't work. My eyes caught hold of Campbell's, and I saw reflected there what he had gone through the day before. Alone at the Holister farm, going from room to room, from old people to middle-aged people, to teenagers, to children and their canine defenders, following the river of blood, part of him feeling responsible for not having stopped the killer before it got to them, part of him not wanting to see what was there before his eyes. As I suddenly went cold sober, he whispered, so as not to be heard by the approaching truckers and Happy Holland employees:

"I know how you feel, sir, but people are coming. We're going to have to tell them something."

"Got'cha."

It wasn't much of a response, but it was all he needed to hear. Knowing I was on the metaphysical mend, he shut his door and marched around the truck to head off those approaching, buying me a handful of seconds to finish pulling my head out of my ass. Wiping my face on my coat sleeve, I threw open my door and went back out into the bracing air, marching straight for the now almost ignored crime scene.

While I did so, Campbell did a smartly professional job of keeping everyone back. Sliding neatly into the cop persona I've hated so often, he didn't have to tell anyone a goddamned thing, and he didn't. One by one, those gathering were dismissed by the force of his will, and the blunt reality that whatever it was that had brought us screaming into the loading area, neither one of us was going to share the secret.

While he handled the tourists, I got down on my hands and knees and began to study the ground. It didn't take more than a few seconds for me to see I was right. I tried moving around, looking at the long dried blood from different angles, but it didn't matter. I was right.

It was easy for me to see why I was the only one to notice what I had. I was the last person to examine that site, as well as the one behind the Gore Center Village. What I had noticed hadn't been there when Peterson and Wiffalon had done their jobs. Indeed, neither coroner had been to both places. But I had, and after a long enough time for things to start happening.

By the time I had given up trying to disprove the two plus two formula, someone higher up the Happy Holland ladder than Ralph Jenks had come across the lot in his shirt sleeves to find out what all the bother was about. He was just getting into it with Campbell when I finally staggered back to my feet. Realizing that, oddly enough, I was the only person who had a chance at keeping a lid on things, I shouted:

"Gentlemen, please—a word." Not seeing Jenks or anyone else I'd met so far since I'd come to the land of wind and frost, I said, "First, let me apologize for our dramatic entrance. My fault entirely. I know the deputy and I have no jurisdiction here, but you see, until yesterday, no one had really examined both crime scenes." My little announcement worked, breaking the man everyone else was treating as the top dog off from the pack. I focused all my attention upon him immediately to keep him moving toward the bloody patch while Campbell continued holding the others back.

"They were separate cases, you understand. Tragic, but that's how these things sometimes happen."

"Things," the top dog barked. "What things?"

Deferring to his rank had cooled the guy down. Playing to his natural desire to remain in charge, I had intimated that I was going to share information with only him. Now I had to actually come up with some. Going with one of my strengths, lying to authority figures, I told him quietly:

"I'm going to come right to the point. I've noticed the possibility—the *possibility*, mind you—of a potentially contagious agent here." As the man's eyes went wide, I lowered my voice even further, adding, "now, understand this is just a guess. But, we have to make certain—we have to be sure."

"What do we have to do?"

I liked this unknown guy, shivering in his shirt sleeves. He didn't come off nearly as afraid as he did sincerely wanting to do his duty. Continuing to whisper, I told him:

"All we need do is make certain that no one disturb the crime scene for a few more hours. I've already looked and it seems that no trucks have rolled over the area. That's good. If we can just keep it that way, as I said, just for a few more hours .. safety, until we can give the all clear... you understand?"

The temperature seemed to be dropping by the second. I was grateful, for I was certain the weather was keeping the guy focused on me. Instead of wondering who I was and what authority I might have, and demanding a lot of useless answers that would only have wasted time, wanting to get back inside made him a lot more agreeable. He gave Campbell and me his word no one or nothing would get within fifty feet of the crime scene until he heard from us. I thanked him as profusely as I knew how. He bought my performance, but then, as far as I knew, I really wasn't acting.

As Campbell and I got back into his truck, he asked if things were as bad as I had been thinking. I assured him they were. Just as he began asking what we should do next, his two-way radio commanded our attention. In our haste, neither of us had thought to let Jeeter know we had arrived.

"My fault, sheriff," I shouted. "And I'll make this as brief as I can. I think I've found something. Something no one is going to like. Can you meet us out at Rafe Holister's?" When he said that he could, I added:

"I'm sorry about this, Will. I know if there's anything you don't need, is crazy Carl Kolchak setting you up to look the fool in front of the national press. But, that's why I'm taking all the blame and keeping everything to myself. And you can thrown me in your jug if this all turns out to be nothing and I'll be happy to just sit back and rot there." I let a long moment of silence go by, then asked:

"Deal?"

"I should have known any man with as little self-regard as to buy Carl Esposito's coat was going to be nothin' but trouble." I could tell by the relief spreading across Campbell's face that Jeeter was in. Taking my own deep breath, I thanked the sheriff, then shut up while he cussed out his deputy for not keeping in touch. Campbell took the lecture in stride, starting his truck and getting it into gear at the same time. Then, once the two had signed off one from the other, he asked:

"Rafe Holister's?"

"And don't spare the siren." ●

CHAPTER SEVENTEEN

"Well, the fat's in the fire now."

Jeeter was waiting for us on the front porch of the Holister farm. Fantastically, there were some fifteen other vehicles there besides the sheriff's cruiser. Mobile feed vans from six different stations were jockeying for space, drivers cursing one another fluently with both words and hand gestures. The rest of the traffic jam was comprised from members of the advance wave of that rental fleet Jeeter had mentioned earlier.

"I'm thinking," Campbell said to me quietly, "that 'bout now Will's no longer much of a happy camper."

From the look of things before us, the deputy had hit on the understatement of the new millennia. Even from back where the snarl of cars had forced us to park, it was fairly obvious the house was still off-limits to the press. As Campbell and I tried to nonchalantly make our way through the throng, it was also evident the mood on both sides of the yellow tape was growing ugly. Nodding my head in agreement, I told Campbell:

"Oh, I do believe you're right about that one."

The sheriff's point was that due to the severe damage done to the individuals inside the house, the recovery team had not yet finished gathering the human remains. Finally, when one of the reporters made a comment about small town inefficiency, Jeeter blew his stack.

"Listen to me, you slick-backed peckerwood. If you're lookin' for me to do a little dance of apology for the fact this town hasn't learned as much about graft and theft so it can climb up out of the shit on the backs of the poor like that rat-hole you're from, you'll be standin' there lookin' one long, goddamned time." Bending down under the police tape, Jeeter strode forward toward the reporter in question, face red, eyes narrowed, shouting:

"You miserable little turd, a family got tore to pieces in there—can you even understand what that means? Human beings, torn up into stew meat--human flesh thrown about, chewed up and spit out--and you, you disgusting maggot, you can't wait to get in there and start stompin' on their bodies? You make me sick."

Luckily for Campbell and myself, the crowd had so concentrated on the sheriff's outburst, and with trying to get shots of his deputies stepping in between him and his target, that none of them stopped to wonder who we were. Granted, to them Campbell was just another deputy. But I know the newshound mind, and if any of them had realized that one of their own was moving through the lines, it was not beyond belief to picture them rushing the building.

To make certain such didn't happen, Jeeter turned angrily on his heel and followed us up the front stairs, then hustled the two of us inside the door, leaving his three other deputies outside to maintain order. Once he had us away from big ears, however, he wheeled on me and snapped:

"All right, and this had better be good, 'cause that bunch out there is ready to serve me up for dinner--Jeeter tartar--so spill it. What the hell did you find that's worse than the fact that the son'-va bitch that did all this is still on the loose?"

"Give me just a minute, Will," I said, my head turned toward the living room. "It might be better, looking out on the porch. I really don't know for sure... it's just ..."

And then I saw it. When I'd been out at the loading area of Happy Holland, it had been such a seemingly normal thing, part of such an ordinary sight I hadn't paid it the slightest mind. Hidden in plain sight, as Conan Doyle would've put it. Seeing it again behind the Gore Village Center, however, had made me wonder, made me just curious enough to take a closer look. Terrified at what I was thinking, hoping to God I was wrong, I'd shanghaied Campbell and made the mad dash back to Two Hollows where I only became more convinced that I was right.

"Hey, you listen to me, Kolchak, I've been in touch with every police department, state and local, and with every sheriff's office as well as the feds from one end of this state, and West Virginia, to the other. We got no new murders yet, but if this guy sets to chompin' again, we gotta be ready."

"I know, I know ..."

"Don't you put me off, mister," Jeeter snapped. His hand on my shoulder, he spun me around so he could look me in the eye as he screamed, "people are scared around here—you got me? They're terrified some maniac the size of a truck is goin' to rip them and everyone they love into little bitty meatballs. We've had three families pick up and leave town--already!"

"I understand people are frightened, sheriff ..."

"Did I say anything about 'frightened?' That's a goddamned small word for what people are around here. They're shittin' their pants is what people are doin' around here." Jeeter stopped for a breath, then waving his hand across the horizon, he said:

"This town of mine, the people in it--those people aren't scared; they are one hundred percent terrified--they are out of their minds with fear, and if you want the truth, I'm one drink and a kick in the ass from joinin' them."

"Will, please," I said, putting my hands up defensively. Trying to calm my own voice, not wanting to send him any further over the line, I said, "Look, as long as I'm in town, I'm just as big a target for whatever it is crawling around out there in the night as anyone else, so let me assure you--I'm just as scared as anybody you might name. In fact, at this point, I'm probably more scared than anyone."

My words--or maybe it was the look in my eyes, whatever—something about me gave Jeeter pause. Still steaming, still shaking, he forced himself to step back and take a moment to pull himself together. Sliding his hat off his head in a clumsy manner, he folded it under his arm, then dropped his voice down to a regular level.

"All right; if I say I've made the trip back from crazy, will you explain to me what it is you think you've found before I buy myself a return ticket?"

I nodded, motioning for the sheriff and Campbell to come and join me in the living room. Getting them to kneel down next to me on the floor, I pointed to one of the thicker patches of blood. It had pooled within the ridges of a knot-weave throw rug. As they looked at it, wondering what I was up to, I asked:

"Notice anything peculiar, there, in the blood? Or should I say, on it?" The pair stared for a couple of seconds, not getting what I was trying to point out. I knew it was subtle, knew it was beyond obvious, but I was desperate for one of them to see it without me having to say anything. Finally, Campbell offered:

"You, you don't mean those, like little green flecks there, do you?"

"Even if you don't," said Jeeter, craning his neck, leaning forward, fascinated, "what the hell is that?"

"I think...," I started, taking a deep swallow, sudden fear gripping my spine, "I think it's moss."

"Moss?" Both men repeated the word in unison. While Campbell went in for his closer look, the sheriff turned and asked, "Carl, what the hell do you mean, moss?"

"Out at Happy Holland..." I said, paused, got hold of myself and then continued, "on the blood. There's moss growing. But, it's like here. It's in the cracks. When I was first out there I didn't think anything of it. Moss, growing in cracks--big deal. Hell, I didn't even notice it to think about it.

"But then, at the Gore Center, I saw the same thing. Moss. Growing in the cracks. But, it's not."

"What the hell's that mean?"

"I mean, and understand me here, I've seen this now at all three crime scenes, and what I've seen, it's thinnest here, and it's thickest at the first..."

"Yeah, yeah, go on."

"What I'm trying to tell you is," I paused again, trying to say what I had to say without sounding as insane as I felt, "it's not moss that's growing in cracks that blood got spilled on. I'm saying I've looked at it, and I've pulled it up, and it's not moss that's growing in the ground. The roots aren't in the soil. They're just in the blood."

"What?"

"The moss, Will, it's growing in the blood--it's rooted in the blood. It's eating the goddamned blood." ●

CHAPTER EIGHTEEN

Things seemed much more exciting that night at The Green Circle than the night before. Of course, there's nothing like an influx of a few hundred people into a town of a few thousand to jam up the local amenities. I was there with LuAnn again, but unlike the night before every table was filled as well as the bar. It was a big day in Gore, and the Green Circle was experiencing something which was only supposed to happen there on Mother's Day; its waiting lounge was in use.

There they all were—cable, network and print, divergent brothers, the bunches of them jammed together--bare elbow to Armanied elbow to elbow patch--all so chuckling happy to see each other. Waiting for their tables, drinking like sailors, joyously smoking in public, it was a time for reminiscing--

Remember that night in Iraq? Oh, God, they were dyin' like flies, weren't they?

And another round of laughter rocked the chandeliers of The Green Circle as old friends frolicked, talking of disasters and suicides and mass graves as if they were one long string of parties—which sadly, for the outsiders gathered under the merry roof of the Green Circle that night, they were.

Don't get me wrong. It takes one to know one. I was there once. From when I was near the top back in the Apple, all the way to the bottom during my days in Las Vegas, I thought the world was one big disappointment that was really only kept interesting by whatever I was doing at the moment. Ink gets in your blood, and disdain welcomes you as a constant companion.

And, if you think I could work a disregard for the man in the street in those days, they make more money on cable and local stations than most print guys ever dreamed of; the networks dwarf them. We were all one worse than the next. Anyone who thinks pouring money on ego is ever a good idea, as my uncle Gustav Kolchak would say, "this is someone you might not want to let play with matches."

But back at the bottom when I spent my own forty days wandering in the desert, I met a man who, through a disdain so monumental it made my own seem like some form of unbridaled compassion, showed me a world beyond most people's comprehension. From that moment on, somehow, no matter where I went, what I did, what kind of life I tried to live, I was haunted by another often quoted line, this one not coined by Uncle Gustav; "you can't go home again."

I looked around the room, at those who could witness the suffering of others and still find humor in it, and I hungered for those days, back when I was just a normal guy. I had a good life then--even in Vegas. I worked when I wanted to; I lived in an exciting town. Sexy women found me attractive--mentally stimulating in a twilight world of gangsters, corporate lawyers and the endless parades of compulsives, losers and freaks. I took advantage of such a fact. As often as I could.

I drank until dawn on the nights I didn't have companionship. It didn't matter. I didn't have to shave for my job. I didn't have to keep my tie tied, or wear one at all. I drove a big car that guzzled great quantities of gas, ate steak and lobster dinners at the casinos that cost pennies and basically felt on top of the world.

Since I'm quoting the greats, I'll add one more. They say you never know what you have until you lose it. Well, let me tell you, truer words were never spoken.

Whenever I thought about the past, it didn't usually hit me that hard. But then, working for the **Dispatch**, I didn't usually end up in social settings with other reporters, let alone network people. There were anchor men in The Green Circle that night. The waitresses were spending every spare second they had calling friends and relatives to let them know local celebrities and those from far away were in the restaurant. Most were given instructions to call others.

That night The Green Circle was merely jammed—extra tables were out, the bar full, the lounge in use. The next night it would be a madhouse. And in the back of their minds, the new arrivals realized exactly what kind of a stir they were making, and they fed off it, were delighted by it. I could see it in their eyes, and I just plain missed that feeling.

The crowd is never on my side. Don't take that the wrong way. That's not my way of whining "oh, please feel sorry for poor little Carlie." Don't worry about me. I'm use to it. What I've learned to live with is that the crowd can't afford to be on my side. They can't handle it. And, you know why? Because half the time anymore, I'm thinking I can't handle it.

Just like those in the crowd remembering the Truth or Dare session everyone had the weekend they were all stuck in Orlando after the Challenger exploded, grinning like mischievous children, I had seen it all. I was hard. I was indifferent. Chop off another head, execute another planeload of innocents, cover babies in lava, let brothers kill brothers, kill mothers, kill themselves, it didn't matter to any of us. Haven't you heard?

We've seen it all.

And then, like I said, there was that man in the desert. And suddenly I knew more than anyone else. I'd been shocked by a horror so far beyond any I'd ever been exposed to I lost my veneer; lost it? It was peeled away, cast away--flung to oblivion in a heartbeat. What I saw, was forced to do, it was impossible to remain unaffected. Most newspeople are the way they are because they've seen all death has to offer, and thus become immune to death's power to frighten.

But me, that much wasn't good enough for me. No, I had to go and learn that your life wasn't all you have to lose. I had to go and learn that we all have souls. That there are things who want more than your life, that there are things who want our eternal spirits-- our very essence.

I arrived at the bar a lot earlier than when I had arranged to meet LuAnn. First off I knew there'd be a crowd, and I knew that production assistants and the like would be making reservations early. Second, after the day I put in, I had a lot of drinking to catch up on. I got a table before they were all gone and I started downing Scotch at a smooth pace. By the time LuAnn arrived, I was as smooth as they come.

Thus, when the poor Ms. Hildebergen arrived, I was in no shape to be subtle. I had started drinking because I wanted to put the nightmare building in the back of my brain out of sight for the moment. I just wanted to look at her, into her eyes, and forget. Forget about crime scenes and torn-to-shreds babies. Forget about scores of slaughtered animals, their bodies ripped apart, heaped together. Forget about blood-drinking plants. Just for a couple of lousy hours.

But surrounded by my peers, watching them enjoy themselves, I found myself growing cold and bitter. With each drink, I discovered I was falling more and more in line with Christ's way of thinking when he petitioned his father to "let this cup pass."

This exciting new, "why me" state of mind had definitely changed the atmosphere between myself and the wonderful woman who clothed me when I was cold. Sensing the same thing I was, but not having any idea what was causing it, LuAnn asked me what was wrong. Being as much of a chump as most men, I went ahead and told her. ●

CHAPTER NINETEEN

"It's not you. Nothing to do with you," I told her, one drunken hand pointing alternately toward LuAnn, then off into space. "It's this damn story. Damn, miserable story-that's what's getting to me."

"You," she said, her tone half-sympathetic, half-mocking, "the great Carl Kolchak? I didn't think that was possible."

I must have looked hurt. Her hand came cutting across the table, her fingers folding over mine so gently their warmth made me shudder. Human contact is something I sometimes find myself in short supply of--most of the time that's the way I like it. But, there, in the Mayberry-like setting of Gore, I was beginning to want to gather up all the human contact I could—especially from one person in particular.

I emptied myself out to her right then and there. The waiter brought her a drink so she could begin the futile task of trying to catch up to me, and I told her what I was feeling. I expressed myself quite vividly, I believe. I base that assessment on the way the look on her face continued to change.

Bit by bit, I gave her the entire, gruesome, terrible story. I related inspecting the crime scenes, one after another, gave her a lot more detail on the Holister place than I'd put into my articles. And then, then I told her about the moss. The hideous, monstrous moss.

"So, were you right," she asked, her face trying not to blanch, her eyes pretending fear wasn't eating at their corners, "was it really growing in the blood, off the blood? Feeding on the blood?"

I nodded weakly, finishing the drink in my hand as I did so. She sat back in her chair, her face showing that she was puzzling over what I said, trying to make sense of it. Noble cuss that I am, I volunteered an explanation.

"We called in the coroner, not the one from over in West Virginia, that Peterson fellow. Not him. Not that I don't trust Peterson—he's okay. But no, we called in the local coroner... ah, Wiffalon. He's not quite as interested in getting his name in the paper ..."

Of course, my speech wasn't nearly that clear. I believe I was calling the local coroner Whip-along, but LuAnn was patient and willing to struggle through to get the whole story. Most people probably would. It was pretty fascinating.

Jeeter left Campbell in control at the Holister farm. Until the recovery team was finished, no one was getting inside. As far as the law was concerned in Gore, all photos from that particular crime scene could be gotten through dealing with my superiors at the *Dispatch*. After that, we met Wiffalon at Happy Holland. He went over the site and reached the same opinion I had even faster than I did.

After that, he took a sample which he not only capped firmly, but then taped shut as well. After that, he told the yogurt boys to get shovels and ten gallons of gasoline. When they did so, he had the earth turned near the pavement for several yards. After that, he had the crime scene doused in gasoline as well as the section of ground where the miscellaneous drop of blood might have been flung. When one of the Happy Holland people asked what he wanted done next, he cursed:

"What in Hell do you think I want done next, you pea-brain? Burn it. Burn it all."

They did, and I swear I saw colors within the flames I have never seen anywhere else. You'll find blues in gas flames, sure. And I've seen every shade of red and orange in campfires, burning buildings, and the like. But there in that parking lot, I saw green flames, and I saw purple ones. And I saw flecks of black, pure ebony fire that ravaged those around it.

When the black flames began to hiss, the ground actually steamed, and I wasn't the only one who saw it. Eyes went wide throughout the crowd, and most of the yogurt boys found excuses to get back to work. They're lucky they did. After they left, as the fire began to hit its zenith, sound came up off the bubbling pavement and out of the hissing earth. It was a growling whisper every one of us wanted to blame on the wind—every one of us knowing we were lying.

Wiffalon was the strongest of the three of us. He congratulated the Happy Holland people on keeping the area clear, on having the good sense to wait until they had official clearance to re-enter the area, and for being so helpful right then and there. He hinted that they had done the community a great service, that most likely they had just helped prevent a major epidemic from breaking out in town. He was, of course, wonderfully mysterious, cautioning the yogurt boys to secrecy.

Then, when we were all back in Jeeter's patrol car, he unlimbered his flask which I fondly remembered from the day before and he sucked down a third of its contents, asking as he handed it over to me:

"Think this will make you feel any better?"

"I'm damn and truly willing to find out," I told him, and took my own massive swallow. Surprising us, Jeeter stretched his hand out, letting us know he had just officially relieved himself of duty for the rest of the day.

The tale of the Gore Center Village went quickly. We went, Wiffalon looked, took another sample, and we burned the hell out of the area. Since it was all pavement, we didn't have any digging to do. No, we merely had to brace ourselves for our next stop.

LuAnn, I give her credit, though her lovely brown eyes were wide and there was no doubt I was scaring her half to death, I saw no doubt within them. She believed me, and she was worried about me--about me and herself and everyone around her. You could see it there, which made me all the crazier for her.

Until that very instant, I had not realized how close to the brink I had wandered, how little I was caring if I fell over its black and jagged edge. But then, seeing that trust in my words, that belief I'd been searching for so desperately, I discovered all the feelings I'd found kindling between us suddenly rushing into a massive inferno. "Love" is a dangerous word, and I've never really been a man who likes danger very much, but I looked at those lovely fingers holding mine, holding onto me—securing me to this world--and I found myself suddenly wondering if I couldn't stand at least that much danger in my life.

In an attempt to find out, I told her the rest. At the Holister place Jeeter and Wiffalon plowed through the now, even-larger crowd with the subtlety of the bulls of Pamplona. The attention they attracted made it relatively easy for me to sneak up to the side of the house where I was let inside by Campbell. Jeeter had radioed that little bit of strategy ahead, just as he had radioed instructions for us to be met by a couple of canisters of gasoline at the Gore Center.

Inside Wiffalon examined the blood and once again found the same growths. He took another sample, then went to the kitchen to clean his tools the same way he had at the first two sites--in fire. Jeeter laid down the law about anyone going near any of the blood spots with the slightest trace of green on them, the coroner backing up his insinuations of possible plague.

"After that," I told LuAnn, my voice falling into whisper as the waitress arrived with our dinners, "the three of us headed to Wiffalon's office where he could give his samples a closer examination."

We stopped talking, of course, as our meals were laid out. I don't remember what we had. Except for the Scotches. I remember plenty of those. Not feeling very hungry, I asked LuAnn if we could eat and get out of the restaurant--away from the crowd and the noise, and all the happy chatter. Not feeling very peckish herself, LuAnn nodded shakily to show her agreement.

We ate as much as we were going to very quickly, which wasn't much. It was a waste of food, and of the ***Dispatch's*** limited resources. Ask me how much I cared. All I wanted to do was to get out of The Green Circle and into a dark, safe hole where I could spill the rest of my guts to LuAnn.

She drove my rental car into the parking lot of Motel 1,2,3! very soon thereafter. LuAnn was shaken, frightened and somewhat in shock. She drove because the polite word for what I was would be drunk. We lead one another inside and made it to the beds. She sat me on the edge of one, then went and started a pot of coffee going in the room's little four-cup coffee maker. As it perked and sputtered, I told LuAnn the rest of what had happened.

I did it to share everything with someone I was falling for as hard and fast as things can fall. I did it to let her know there would be no secrets between us. I did it so she could get a handle on things, so that once she knew everything that was happening she could finally relax a bit--put shock and despair and fear behind her.

Really, after all this time, you'd think I'd learn. ●

CHAPTER TWENTY

"What do you mean, Carl," she asked me. The coffee had just just finished brewing and LuAnn had just finished pouring me a cup. I'd asked her to make it sweet. I don't know why. She was stirring the end product as she crossed the room, asking me, her voice trembling, "how could there be more to tell? What else could there possibly be to this?"

"You," I stumbled over the simple word, still slightly slurring my speech. Almost laughing, stopping myself from crying, I worked at pulling my miserable self together, then said, "you have no idea."

I took the coffee from her and sipped at it carefully. Drunk as I was, I still understood what the sight of steam meant. The stuff was bitter, despite sugar and artificial sweetener, but I figured with the amount of damage I'd done myself that day, I was lucky I could taste anything at all.

Getting down a couple more tiny sips, I put the cup on the nearest nightstand, the scalding heat of its brew making my tongue and throat feel a bit more normal. I closed my eyes as hard as I could, trying to clear them, then excused myself for a trip to the bathroom. I didn't need to close the door; I was simply after the sink. Eight or nine double-handed splashes of water in the face later I returned to my bed, fortified myself with a few more sips of coffee, then returned to my tale.

"It's what Wiffalon found... what, what he found in the moss."

I motioned for LuAnn to sit down across from me on the other bed. She did, reaching for my hands. I took hers, grateful for their touch. I wondered if she had any idea how much that small gesture meant to me, how much it kept me going--kept me in one piece. Staring hard at her, through the booze and the self-pity, I somehow found the strength to untwist the knots in my tongue and get it working once more.

"He put it under the microscope," I told her, "gave the stuff a good hard look. He cursed a lot while he studied it, constantly talking about what he was seeing not making any sense."

Not wanting to, but figuring it was for the best, I released one of LuAnn's hands for a moment and grabbed up my coffee cup. It wasn't much cooler, but I managed to gag down a few more sips. Feeling a slight bit better, I went back to my story.

"He cut a few pieces in sections, called in a lackey... rattled off some tests he wanted done. Don't remember what he said. Didn't make any sense... just science stuff--"

I was wandering and I knew it. Pardoning myself for a moment, I shut my lips and eyes and shook my head as hard as I could. Yes, I thought, I'd put more than my share of Scotch and a few of his friends into me that day, but I could usually handle such excesses better.

You're getting old, the back of my mind whispered. I didn't argue. Feeling a little bit more together, though, I hurried back to my tale before I started succumbing to the inevitable.

"No sense in dragging it out. Jeeter and I cooled our heels for a couple of hours. Then Wiffalon finally stopped trying to make sense of what he was looking at, and just told us what he was seeing. He had to tell us twice."

"Why?"

"Because," I said quietly, trying to prepare her for when I told her the same things, "we didn't believe him."

LuAnn trembled despite herself. I could see it in her eyes, feel it through her hands. She knew she was going to hear something she didn't want to hear, or I thought, maybe it was more. Perhaps she had already heard all she could bear. I had told her in as much detail as she wanted to hear about the carnage at the Holister's, and as I kept talking, she knew I was going to tell her something monstrous was behind it.

Well, I told myself, if that's what she's thinking, she's right.

"What did he tell you, Carl?"

"He said the moss wasn't just moss. That it wasn't completely moss. Or... I mean... that it wasn't all plant life."

"What?"

"The reason the moss could feed on blood, and Wiffalon was about as positive as you can be that it was feeding on blood, was that it wasn't completely plant life. Yeah, yeah, he went into a whole long thing about how some plants hunt insects and fish and even small mammals, but he said it wasn't anything like that. This wasn't a plant that hunted for blood, that really, it wasn't a plant at all. It was something new, something else ..."

"What are you saying, Carl," LuAnn demanded, her voice frightened and growing shrill. "Just what are you telling me?!"

"This stuff, this thing, growing in the blood, its DNA is made up from plant and mammal DNA. It's some kind of hybrid, one that shouldn't be able to exist."

As LuAnn sat before me dumbly, her mind rolling over what I had said again and again within her mind, I took the moment to take a long pull of my coffee. It hadn't grown that much cooler, but I wanted it, needed it. Licking drops of the bitter crap off my lips, I told her:

"He showed us under the microscope; there was actually hair growing up out of the stuff. Green, curling like regular moss, but it was hair... hair."

LuAnn's face went pale, the irises of her brown eyes retreating to pin points. I felt horrible, knowing I'd upset her for no better reason than to make myself feel better. It pained me inside to know I'd done such a thing to anyone, let alone a woman for whom I felt the way I felt about LuAnn.

As she sat there, staring at me, I took a moment to swallow another slug of coffee. I was fading fast, falling into a slurring sleep despite the brew I'd had already. It wasn't all that surprising to me. After all, one cup of coffee, stacked against a massive amount of alcohol, slugging it out in a belly with eight bites of dinner trying to referee, what a surprise that I found myself yawning, falling toward the bed. I apologized to LuAnn in the manner of the typical slobbering drunk.

I told her how much I cared about her, told her I couldn't understand why I was in such bad shape, that usually I held my liquor a lot better. She told me to be quiet, to not worry about such things. Moving next to me, she hugged me gently, whispering softly:

"Carl, you need rest. I don't think it's the drinking. It's stress. All you've seen. Not just here. It's everything, from Vegas on, and it's catching up with you here."

"But," I said groggily, needing her so, "it's not right. Shouldn't leave you... never want to leave ..."

He-man that I was at that moment, I couldn't even finish my

sentence, let alone guard my lady fair. As I faded in and out, mostly out, I felt her slip my jacket off, then ease me back onto the pillow. She loosened my tie, then pulled it free and undid the buttons of my shirt. She undid my belt and removed it, as well as my shoes and my socks. I felt like the luckiest man in the world, and like the world's biggest moron for failing her so utterly.

Her only response to my passing out on her was to tuck me in and then kiss me on the forehead. I know I was awake for that. It was too wonderfully reassuring, too warm and too perfect to have been a dream. No, although the state I was in was one of being just barely awake, as long as she remained, I managed to maintain my focus. I watched her slip her coat back on, her hat and her gloves, gather up her bag. Then, just before she went to the door, she bent close and whispered:

"Sweet dreams, Carl Kolchak."

I know I heard those words. I know they were real, because I remember to what a nightmarish extent her wish for me did not come true. ●

CHAPTER TWENTY-ONE

"Who do you think you are, Carl Kolchak?"

The question came out of the air, booming and dark and terrible. The sound of it terrified me, made my blood crunch into ice, turned my spine into rubber. I didn't know who or what was doing the questioning, but I was frightened nonetheless.

"Who do you think you are, Carl Kolchak?"

Having the hideous voice shout at me again did nothing to put me at ease. I turned my head in all directions, but could not see anyone. My vision filled with the sight of far-away mountains being blasted and dashed by purple slashes of lightning. Scarlet dust swept along the ground around my feet, blowing in an opposite direction from the clouds that raced across the sky.

"I'm dreaming," I heard myself say aloud.

"What if you are?" The hideous voice rattled ominously down from the sky, the foul stench of it choking me as it warned, "this is your last chance, Carl Kolchak--tell me. Tell us all. Who do you think you are?!"

The voice forced me to my knees, then toppled me completely, the power of it sucking the very life from my body. I struggled to rise, threw everything I had to just prying myself up from the ground. There was nothing in me of defiance or fearlessness. I was too confused by everything to even begin to unravel what was happening to me. Yes, I knew I was dreaming, but it was like nothing I had ever experienced before.

I've had bad dreams in my time. And I've had them after and during some of those periods when I was tracking stories of what most people would call a "fictional" nature. But, none of them had ever been anything like this one.

"You have been judged a fool, Carl Kolchak."

I didn't like the sound of that. Not because I had any misconceptions of how I was perceived in the world, but because the way the words were being hurled at me, I had a feeling the sentence for being a fool in that particular dream was going to be something extremely unpleasant.

Gathering what strength I could find, I turned around and ran in what I hoped was somehow the opposite direction. It was a flat out run through the swirling dust, one that started me panting after only fifty yards. In another fifty I was gasping for air. Another found me staggering, reeling forward, blinking sweat out of my eyes.

"A fool because you seek to escape the obvious ..."

Hands reached up out of the vast and stretching plane, grabbing at my legs. I kicked my way through them, jumped on fingers, dodged when I could.

"A fool refuses to accept the inevitable ..."

I wished desperately that I could wake myself up. Not only was this dream unlike any I'd ever had before, but from those nightmares I'd experienced in the past, once I realized that I was having a dream, I'd always been able to wake myself up. But not this time. No, for some reason I could not comprehend, I was in the grasp of my subconscious and it was not letting go for a while.

"And a fool is what you are, Carl Kolchak, a blind and gibbering puppet, one surrounded by trees who cannot find a forest."

"Leave me alone," I screamed. "I didn't do anything to you. I don't deserve this!"

"Didn't you?" The monstrous voice hissed. "Don't you? Think about it. Ask your old friends."

I wondered what the voice meant, but only for a moment. As I stood on the barren plane, suddenly all around me shadows began to form in the distance. One by one they took shape and began to move forward on me. One by one I recognized them. It didn't take long before I was screaming.

The first one to reach me, as anyone who knows my career might expect, was that man who taught me so much in the desert. Janos Skorzeny, the vampire, the undead thing that blasted my world view and self-image to dust merely by existing. He was the first to turn my life inside out, and he was the first to find me that night. He walked up to me silently, eyes gleaming with hatred. I tried to run, threw my hands before my face, and watched as in slow motion he drew his hand back, then thrust it forward and drove it through my chest.

I shrieked, closing my eyes against the pain. When I opened them once more, my arms were being pulled in different directions, one by a merciless suit of armor I'd once consigned to the rubbish heap, the other by a black and horrible set of tentacles extending forth from a crack in reality. Holding me fast, I struggled as others came forth for their chance to wound me.

The parade seemed endless.

A large, cracked mirror floated past me and a bloody clawed hand reached out of it and tore my face away. Flaming bodies and a terrible black dog ravaged me, followed by an ancient corpse wrapped in bandages and a snake-headed female who fell to chewing on my chest, pulling away never-ending strips of my flesh. They had plenty of help.

Ghosts and witches, demons and aliens, balls of pure energy and winged lizardmen fell upon me, each consuming me, each lavishing my dream body with a savage hatred which made my conscious body shiver despite the fact I had set the heat in my room to 82 degrees and kept it there since I'd arrived. After a while I ceased struggling; I had nothing left to give despite the fact my memory could find plenty who wanted to take.

My dreamself lay in a ever-widening pool of my own blood and urine and feces. My nose dripped great festoons of mucus which stuck to everything. I cried pitifully, but it brought me no respite, garnered me no mercy. The onslaught continued, demons and yetis and more falling upon me repeatedly, reducing me finally to bones, and then merely nerve endings.

And then, all my tormentors fled the scene, disappearing into the scarlet dust, flying away into the distant mountains, scattering like leaves in a gale. All my tormentors, that is, that had already scarred and mutilated me. As the very little bit of me that remained bled and cried and puked, two final shadows stretched forward out of the darkness, the mere shade of them burning my nightmare-abused body.

I knew I should know them. Their look, their smell, the sounds they made, all of it was familiar to me. The one was broad and silent, the other, wild and snorting. Both came for me, one with fangs, the other with strangling hands. They trampled me, and then they doused me in a noxious liquid. Startled, my dreamself tried to make sense of this latest attack. It did not have to wait long.

Standing back, the things somehow created fire from nowhere and hurled it at me. That was when I realized I was coated in gasoline. My skin began to boil and peel from my body. With no time for tears, I screamed loud and long. I screamed there in my dream from the depths of my soul. I screamed so loudly I finally woke myself up.

For a moment I kept screaming, my hands beating at the flames I had left behind on the other side of nightmare. It took more than a moment for me to realize I was awake. Awake and finally sober, awake and safe from those things from my past seeking to destroy me. And then, as I heard my own thoughts within my head, I realized something else.

Like all people waking from a dream, I felt it rushing away from me, the bits and pieces of it folding back into my subconscious. But, also like anyone else, the part of the dream that was really important to me, that thing I had been using the dream realm to try and tell myself, struggled to stay with me. My subconscious had put two and two together, coming up with five, and insisting it was the answer to what was going on in Gore.

I lay in bed groaning, not certain if it was the night before or my epiphany that was making me do so. I was coming out of one of the worst hangovers I'd ever experienced, one so draining it made me feel I knew what the old timers from the sixties and seventies were talking about when they went on about having a "bad trip." That made me wonder if the idea that had come to me had any validity at all, or if I was merely going insane.

I was just about to attempt the Herculean feat of getting myself out of bed when I finally noticed the man sitting on the other bed--that and the gun in his hand. ●

CHAPTER TWENTY-TWO

Shrieking, I kicked at the blanket and sheet and spread, pushing myself backward, attempting to escape whoever it was that had broken into my room. In less than heroic fashion, I only managed to get myself completely entangled within the sweat-soaked bed covers, wrapping myself up tighter than if I was handcuffed. Considering how much I had perspired while having my nightmares, it was a pretty miserable prison. I finally stopped struggling when I heard the gunman asking:

"How are you feeling, Carl?"

The tone with which the question was asked made me take a moment to listen. The words truly sounded as if they were meant to convey genuine concern. After a final second of terror, my dream-riddled brain started its gears grinding, which allowed a bit of blood to flow through it. The oxygen thus delivered helped me remember that genuine concern generally meant no shouting. Daring to open my eyes the rest of the way, I realized I knew my new roommate.

"Jesus Christ," I cursed, more from amazement than anything else. "What the hell are you doing here?"

My uninvited visitor was one Peter Norman, of the FBI. Seeing me coming to, he slid his automatic neatly into its shoulder holster. Why he had it out in the first place, I forgot to ask. Maybe he was guarding me. Maybe he was making certain it was clean. In all honesty, though, I was glad he put it away. The way my head was throbbing I felt too much like dying to dare ask what someone was doing with a weapon--I might have asked to borrow it.

I looked again, blinking my eyes hard against the early morning crud deposits, making certain I had correctly identified my intruder. Focusing on his face, I relaxed somewhat. If it wasn't Peter Norman, it was a damn fine imitation. Six foot three, or four, blue eyes, lean build, he was a poster boy for the FBI. Norman was only about five years younger than me, but in the kind of shape that probably allowed him to chase women fifteen years younger than me. Those added good looks probably allowed him to catch most of them, too.

I had met him following a story up the California coast late the year before. He and his partner, an unfriendly, weak-chinned female by the name of Linda Boll, had been assigned to watch me, and to determine if I was a liability to one of our government's countless national security secrets. By the time it was all over, I'd managed to help stop the end of the world, which had brought the government begrudgingly onto my side. For a while, at least.

"Need some help?"

I frowned at the government's idea of humor then clawed my way free of my bedding, mumbling all the time. I felt weak, almost feverish, and wondered if my few days in real weather had knocked me out of the leagues of the healthy. Drinking too much can invite such things. Hoping it was all just hangover, I forced my feet to find the floor, then dragged my head upward slowly until Norman and I were no longer at a horizontal/vertical showdown. Skimming my tongue with my teeth, I raked away as much of the guck coating it as I could, then asked again:

"What's the matter? FBI work bad for the hearing? What are you doing here?"

He started to answer but before he could, the door opened and the ever-so-charming Ms. Linda Boll, Norman's partner, let herself into my room, along with a fresh blast of Virginia's version of December. I merely groaned at the sight of her, which prompted Norman to comment:

"See, he's happy to see you, too."

"OOOhhhhh, yum! Now there's a fact that's got me all warm and fuzzy inside," she said, snorting as she did so. Boll was an ungainly woman who knew the fact well and despised anyone else who could figure it out. A ballerina trapped in a lumberjack's body, she was big and strong, with shoulders like a coffee table and thighs I was certain could crush almost any man she wrapped them around. She was just about to make a further comment when my brain went into overtime, force-feeding me an idea I knew instantly had to be correct. Snapping my fingers I pointed at Norman, shouting:

"Jesus Christ! It was you, wasn't it? It had to be. 'Be careful, nothing is as it seems.' You're my friend."

The effort left me groaning. I had begun shaking my finger wildly, pointing at one of them, then the other, but the exertion made my entire body hurt, and I stopped wasting such vast quantities of energy as quickly as I had begun. Tears burst forth from my eyes and I began coughing. My throat was sore, my eyes burning. I cursed Morgan Slate for sending me to the frozen ends of the Earth, then I cursed Tony Vincenzo for letting him. After that I blamed the real culprit for all my woes and cursed myself. As I ran out of air for tirades, Boll came over to me, moving into the spot on the opposite bed her partner had been warming.

"Open your mouth," she ordered. Knowing she could take me three falls out of three, I did as she said. She shone a small flashlight down my throat, then said: "you're not sick."

"Glad to hear it, I guess," I told her. "Although I guess it means I'm getting too old to drink myself to sleep anymore." As I began to work up the courage to stand, she snapped:

"Don't go anywhere."

I didn't. Taking the same flashlight, she shone it in my eyes, yelled at me to keep my eyes open, and then stared into first my left eye, then the right. Using her hand, she pulled the corners of my eyes this way and that, then said:

"Good news, Kolchak; for what's it worth, you can keep on destroying your liver. You're not suffering from the flu or a hangover."

I moved my teeth and tongue around in my mouth, trying to cut through the chalky taste still clinging there. The back of my mind was doing a little dance, grateful for the news that I didn't have to seriously consider limiting my drinking. To quote Santa once more:

"A man's got to do something to keep warm."

But then, as I began to feel almost human again, another part of my brain that had decided to finally wake up and start earning its keep took a look at the last thing Boll had said. Making me take notice she had left something unsaid, I thanked it, then asked:

"If you don't mind telling me, if I'm not sick, or hung over, then why do I feel so miserable?"

Without missing a beat, as if such things happened every day, the woman who has to be the largest female the FBI ever hired turned back to me and said:

"You were drugged." ●

CHAPTER TWENTY-THREE

"What?"

I couldn't believe what had been said. Or at least, I didn't want to believe it. The only person that could have done such a thing was LuAnn, and that made no sense to me whatsoever. Explaining such in a way that got across I wanted an explanation, Norman answered:

"Calm down. There's nothing that says it was your lady friend, Carl. In case you haven't noticed, you've taken quite a high profile in this case. No doubt plenty of varied parties have wondered what you're up to." As I took his advice and grew a bit calmer, he added:

"Look at us. After your flaming torch antics yesterday with Sheriff Jeeter and the local coroner, we were ordered in to make contact with you. We know you; you have a reason to trust us." When I turned toward him and simply snorted, he answered without taking offense:

"Can we agree you have more reason to trust us that most other government officials?" When I gave him that one, he continued, admitting:

"Okay. There's a dozen other departments and agencies and the such, however, who probably have their eye on this case as well. I wouldn't suspect your local fling as much as I would one of them. After all, you just told us you saw her leave. For me, it's a lot easier to believe than someone entered your room after she left, hit you with either a whiff of gas, a soaked cloth to the nose, an injection, you-name-it, and then had a good look at your files, notes, whatever they wanted."

"I don't know," said Boll, smirking, "knowing his type's taste in woman, I vote for the girlfriend."

"You know," I answered, trying to not sound as vindictive as I felt, "you were a lot prettier on TV."

My reference, of course, was to that old television program about the two FBI agents who ran around investigating the supernatural. It still struck me as funny that the agency would put a man and woman together to look into such things, especially a male agent with a female doctor, after that show was on for so long, but who am I to try and understand the way our wonderful government does anything?

Besides, it gave me a great chance to be cruel right back to her. And before you judge me, think about it for a minute, and then tell me you'd have done any different.

"So, Carl," Norman intervened before his partner and I got into one of our full-blown shouting matches, "think you could spend some time filling us in on what went on yesterday?"

Always a sucker for Norman's sense of diplomacy, I agreed. I did ask for a few minutes to take a shower and change. Boll tactfully volunteered to go out for coffee and whatever passed for bagels in Gore. I guess she didn't want to see me naked anymore than I wanted to see her in a similar state. It was a sensible gesture on her part and I made a mental note that I owed her one.

Putting my head under a hot shower that morning ranked up there with the Christmas morning I got my air rifle from my dad. As the steam built around me, I felt a ton of mucus and who knew what else loosen within my head. I held one nostril in and blew, breaking a crust and unleashing a torrent of goo from the other. The resulting relief did much to clear my head, but the feel of the ooze clinging to my fingers only reminded me of the buckets of blood and acres of flesh I'd seen strewn all about me the day before. I let the burning water splash against my chest and scald the outside of me clean. It was going to take a lot more than a simple shower, however, to wash the memory of a houseful of dead bodies from my mind. As I worked past the memory, I felt like I owed Boll more than one simply because she'd told me I could keep drinking.

By the time I was showered and shaved, I felt almost back to normal. A comb through the hair, a clean set of clothes, and I have to admit I was feeling fairly fantastic. Norman said that made sense. Most all of the popular items in the government's current arsenal of knockout drugs, he told me, were designed not to linger in the system.

"Honestly, if you hadn't been so drunk, you probably wouldn't have felt a thing this morning. They either didn't know you'd been drinking so heavily, or didn't care."

"Still," I answered, tying my tie, "what the hell could they have wanted?" Holding up a small electronic device of some design with which I was not familiar, but which did have cables with jacks which I could tell would fit my laptop, he answered:

"One thing they wanted was the contents of your computer. I did a search to see if you'd had an invasive sweep. You did, and in the last twelve hours. I've also had a little look around the place to see if they left you any presents."

Reaching to the desk, he grabbed up a handful of small bits of further electronics. Holding them out before him, he said, "listening devices, as I'm sure you could figure out on your own. In your phone, the motel phone--your cell phone was clean--one in the bathroom, two in here, one near the bed you've been using, the other near the far chair."

"What...?" I didn't finish the question. Mainly because I didn't even know what the question was. Taking pity on me, Norman volunteered:

"All standard government issue. Same thing about the placement. Textbook stuff. You were spooked, Carl. Someone wants to know everything you're doing, who you're guests are, who you're talking to, the whole banana."

At that point Boll returned. She even knocked. In the target-on-my-back state of mind into which I was slipping, I was so happy to see her I decided I now owed her three for the knocking. Norman filled her in on what he'd found while she passed out paper cups of coffee and orders of buttered toast wrapped in napkins.

When I simply stared, she told me to eat, reminding me that no matter how good I might think I felt, she knew more about what I needed than I did. I nodded contritely and started in on the toast. Finishing the first half-slice in two bites and instantly attacking the next one, I decided she was right. I did not decide I owed her four, however. My ego can only take so much in one morning. After I washed down the first piece, I asked:

"So, you pulling all their bugs, does that mean they're going to come back and louse me up again tonight?"

"No way to know. I always carry an Interferer." He flashed another device, explaining, "it shuts off any listening device within a short range area around me. I'll put all their units back before we leave. So basically, if they're only listening to you, they'll think you just didn't get up yet."

"If they're watching you as well," Boll added, "then there's no telling."

I accepted it all as something I couldn't do anything about one way or the other. Deciding it was better if I acted like I didn't know anything and just waited to see what happen, I went back to sucking down my toast and coffee. Having barely eaten anything the day before, then having been hung over and drunk on top of that, my body was screaming at me to keep feeding it. As I did, I asked my new best buddies if they wanted to hear what they had come to hear.

"I think," answered Norman as he started putting the listening devices back in their varied hiding places, "we should do that elsewhere. Whoever's listening is going to expect you to be on your way soon. We're going to clear out of here. What you should do is pretend to wake up, turn on the shower, then say something about meeting Sheriff Jeeter. We'll meet you at that diner in town, Larry's—you know it, right?"

When I confessed to be well-acquainted with the joys of LET LARRY FEED YA, Norman said, "Fine. We'll see you there. It shouldn't take you too long, I even laid out your coat and hat for you while you were in the shower." I looked over at my new coat and my old hat sitting on the bed waiting for me and said:

"Yeah, and just how do you know I was going to wear that hat today?"

"Give us a break, Kolchak," answered Boll in a snide tone, "when did you ever wear any other hat?" I had to give her that one. As I gave her a sad little shrug of defeat, she snapped:

"Just get moving. Get your ass over to the diner, and let's get this over with. You'll give us what you know, and we'll give you what we know, and if you behave your miserable self maybe we'll even fill you in on the news you probably don't have yet." As the pair of them headed for the door, I asked:

"Why, what the hell else has happened around here?"

"The killer struck again last night." ●

CHAPTER TWENTY-FOUR

"Who're your friends, Carl?"

Before I could say anything, Norman introduced himself and his partner by their right names, but as reporters out of Baltimore. It was a good cover. Larry's had become as popular as The Green Circle, filled from one end to the other with news-people of all types. The world's most rationale hippy hadn't taken much notice of them when they'd come in, but once I joined them they became "friends of Carl," which meant they got extra fine treatment. Considering how fine the treatment was at Larry's before we'd become friends, I couldn't imagine how it could get much better, but I was willing to see.

"You folks don't worry about ordering. I'm just going to send one of the girls out with a family style breakfast for you all. Coffee all around?"

Boll asked for tea. Larry made a mental note, and was just about to head back for the kitchen when he stopped himself, then turned and said:

"Hey, Carl, Jeeter was in here earlier, told me to ring him when I saw you. I'll be doing that as soon as I get back into the kitchen... just to let you know... unless..."

I smiled at his left-over sixties paranoia, finding it endearing, to say the least. His hinting pauses were as subtle as a chihuahua in a punch bowl, but remembering that he could just as easily be saving my ass, I told him to go ahead and make the call and send out breakfast for three to which he responded:

"Yeah. He probably just wants to tell you about the new murder and all."

Once Larry was gone, I turned to Norman and said, "Let's get a jump on the sheriff. Why don't you two tell me about the 'new murder and all.'"

Normal proceeded to without hesitation. Apparently two state troopers were attacked during the night while on highway duty. They had made a routine check in, announcing they were going after a car doing over a hundred miles an hour down I-95.

"They caught up to it and pulled it over," Norman told me, "that much had been confirmed by their radio entries to their headquarters. The rest came from on-site investigation."

We paused for a moment as two coffees and a tea were delivered to the table along with a lazy susan-like device holding four different types of syrup and three plates. The girl told us food would start arriving shortly. We thanked her, and then got back down to business.

"Tire marks, foot prints, they showed a normal halt-and-check had been carried out. The officers had approached the car, then all hell had broken loose. The officers were torn to bits, some of the pieces missing this time--supposedly just like at the last crime scene you were tramping over earlier. Even their cruiser was totaled, wrenched apart by something with what's being described in whispers as superhuman strength."

"You said this happened on I-95; isn't that the interstate that runs down along the east coast? Isn't that pretty far from here?"

"Guy who drives over a hundred miles an hour can cover a lot of ground," offered Boll.

"That's true," I agreed, nodding my head. Then, dropping my voice to the lowest whisper I hoped could be heard over the crowd all around us, I added, "but I don't think what we're looking for here could technically be called a 'guy.'"

As our waitress arrived, conversation stopped once more. Behind the girl's back, Boll rolled her eyes while Norman complemented the food, marveling widely over how good everything looked. The girl beamed as if she'd done the cooking herself. I had to admit, Norman was quite the charmer. On the other hand, in his defense, there was a lot to complement coming to the table.

Larry had sent a heap of scrambled eggs in their own hot tray, along with sides of link sausage, bacon, ham slices, grits and home fries. The waitress told us we were supposed to get started, and that pancakes would follow in about fifteen minutes, unless anyone wanted a waffle instead. When we all declined waffles, Norman adding not to make pancakes for him, she told us:

"They're really good waffles. Larry puts pecans in them, covers them with whipped creme. They're awful yummy."

I wondered how she stayed so slim and perky wolfing down such things. I also noted that her description motivated Boll to change her mind and asked for two. I smiled, refusing to make a comment about her never fitting into a size eight if she kept up things like that, merely revising my scorecard to read that I only owed her one. Norman chuckled, and said he might have a couple pancakes, but pleaded for her to tell Larry not to go overboard.

"I hate to waste food," he explained. He said the words as if he'd seen something in his time that made the idea intensely personal, and the girl simply nodded, as if she could tell exactly what that something was. As the waitress left, Boll snapped:

"All right, Kolchak, what the hell do you mean with this, 'not a guy' stuff? This another one of your crackpot internet tabloid specials?" Reaching for the eggs, I dished myself a portion as I reminded her:

"Larry will be coming back, and he's not nearly as burnt as he looks. If we're not eating, we'll be explaining to him why not. Eggs anyone?"

"I'm filling my plate," said Norman. "Talk. What do you have?"

"All I have is a hunch, and I have whoever slipped me that mickey last night to thank for it." Piling on the bacon--Larry only served the thick-sliced kind, the kind that I adore--and a few sausages, some potatoes, and a bit of everything else, just to be polite, I continued.

"I had a dream last night, but it was different than anything that I've ever experienced before. It was like I really was some other place—I mean, I knew I was dreaming, but it felt as if I'd reached some other reality simply by dreaming."

"You talking astral projection?"

"I don't know," I told Norman, "and I'm not sure it's even important. What I'm trying to say is, I found myself searching in my mind through all the weird things I've come across these past few years." I started in on a sandwich made of toast, eggs, bacon and ham, continuing to talk in between bites.

"All the vampires, witches, you name it, I saw them all again. Felt them, touched them, or more to the point, they touched me, tore at me, endless torture kind of thing. Like I said, I really think the booze and drugs put me into some kind of state I could have never reached any other way."

"Fine, Carl—no one's arguing." Norman neatly sliced up a ham steak while he asked, "But what is it that happened in this dream that makes you think you now have some insight into what's going on out here?"

"It was the last two things that attacked me. It was like I had to suffer all the others once more, be reminded about them before I could remember these two."

The pancakes and waffles arrived at that point. We made another fuss over the waitress, sending her away all smiles. After that, I tried to get back to business. Telling my own personal FBI agents that I needed to give them some background, I told them everything that had happened to me since I'd come to where winter was more than just a concept.

I was able to skip over most of what there was to say about the crime scenes—that they already knew. All I really needed to concentrate on was Jeeter and Wiffalon and my own torching of the crime scenes the day before, and why. I told them of the blood-drinking moss, and of its unique DNA. And then I told them what I had been thinking, something so bizarre, so frighteningly unsettling that even I was having trouble believing it.

"A few years back, as you've probably read about, I encountered a werewolf on a ship at sea. Only a little over a month later, I ran into this thing called a peremalfait, a kind of Cajun bogeyman. It's this... well, this thing; it's shaped like a man, but it's made out of moss. Spanish moss, kinda. You know, the stuff that hangs from the trees down South."

"Yes," mumbled Norman, sliding his words around a mouthful of home fries and eggs. "So ..."

"I think..." I started, knowing exactly how idiotic I was about to sound, wondering which mental institution they would take me to, and if I would bother to put up a struggle, "that this killer we're all looking for is, is ..."

"A hybrid," blurted Boll. "I told you!"

I stared, my mouth hanging open. Whether or not food fell out of it I don't know. It wasn't something worth worrying about at the moment. I had been about to say what I thought was going to be the most ridiculous sentence of my life, that I thought somehow, two dead monsters I had personally sent to Hell, or wherever such things go, had mated and given the world a new terror worse than either of them. I had been about to say that, and accept the consequences, only to find that the FBI had it on their chart of standard theories.

I didn't know whether or not to be relieved that I had an ally, or annoyed to have been scooped. I did know I wanted some answers of my own. Mainly how anyone else could possibly have arrived at the same conclusion I had. And, I was just about to start pounding on the table, and demanding those answers, when a smiling Larry arrived with his trusty coffee pot, saying:

"So, who's ready to talk about murder?" ●

CHAPTER TWENTY-FIVE

No sooner had Larry come to the table than we were joined by Jeeter as well. Grabbing a cup from behind the counter, Larry filled it with brew and handed it off to the sheriff who thanked him as he took the empty chair at the table. Eyeing some of the buffet bounty spread before the FBI and myself, he asked Larry to "rustle him up a plate." While the proprietor did so, Jeeter told us all quickly:

"We all need to talk." Looking at Norman and Boll, he asked, "Can one of you distract him while the rest of us throw down on a load of crap?"

Boll volunteered. As Larry returned, she made a comment about how she'd never had such wonderful waffles, and how they must have come from one of the best prepackaging houses in the world. His feathers visibly ruffling, Larry insisted it was his own secret recipe. Cooing that such a wonderful concoction would make a great feature on her network's early morning show, she hustled him off to the kitchen to tell her all about his award-winning waffles. As he passed out of earshot, Norman whispered:

"Don't panic, Carl. Linda and I introduced ourselves to the sheriff earlier in the week when we first arrived in town. Standard procedure, you know." My eyes wide, I just nodded as he turned to Jeeter, asking:

"What's the news, sheriff?"

"Oh, we got fun aplenty brewin' in this neck of the woods," Jeeter answered, "let me tell you. Wiffalon's goin' to be here to meet us. Says he's got somethin' that puts this new killer attack up to question."

"What do you mean," asked Norman. "Or at least, what does he mean? So far it sounds the same as the others."

"And you tellin' me you're buyin' it?" Jeeter let the question hang while he grabbed a few pancakes for himself. Dousing them in blue-berry syrup, he lay a ham steak on top of it all, while barking:

"Like hell you're not. I already got word from a cousin of mine who's State. Says you boys have a team goin' over everythin' out there on 95 right now."

"We might at that," replied Norman with a smile. "But that's standard and you know it. What's Wiffalon think he's got?"

"Not somethin' I wanted to hear over the phone. We'll all find that out together."

"Works for me."

While Boll continued to keep Larry distracted, I caught Jeeter up on everything that had happened, including my being drugged and my room being turned into a recording studio. I also gave him the details on my nightmare, and my even more-crazy-than-usual idea. While he shoveled in mouthfuls of blueberried pancake and ham, Norman backed me up, letting the sheriff know that for what it was worth, the FBI had already come to the same conclusion about the probability of the killer being both non-human and some kind of hybrid. Swallowing a mouthful of breakfast, Jeeter reached for his coffee to wash it down, admitting:

"You won't get any argument out of me. After lookin' through Wiffalon's microscope at that shit... watchin' them little hairy tendrils movin' on their own..." The sheriff shuddered slightly, then took a massive swallow of coffee. Wiping his mouth on the back of his hand, he added:

"Christ sake, Carl. How the hell you stay sane these last few years?" When I tried to just make a joke, he cut me off. His eyes scanning the door to the kitchen, he said:

"Don't blow me off, goddamnit—not about this. I'm serious. This shit's got me rattled, and I'm not ashamed to admit it." Jetter filled his mouth, his hand shaking ever so slightly as he slid his fork back out into the open. Using it as a pointer, he aimed it in my general direction, chewing while he added, "Now you, you seem a reasonably normal enough human being. Most reasonable, normal people, just seein' one of the things you've seen, they'd be needin' a stay at the funny farm. But you, I mean..." He stalled for a long moment, covering his hesitation with a swallow. Then, swinging his fork absently over his plate, his voice dropping to a whisper, he finally asked:

"Je-zuz, Carl ... how do you do it?"

"You have to remember, Will," I told him quietly, "I covered the crime scenes in both New York and Chicago. You see a lot in towns like that. I mean, you walked the length of the Holister place. You were there behind the Gore Center. You count the inside of that barn, and you've seen more death in the past couple days than most people, including most cops, will ever see in their entire lives. You falling apart yet?"

Jeeter went quiet for a moment, obviously rolling what I'd said around within his head. After a bit, he said:

"I guess it all comes down to what you get used to."

"Yeah," I answered, my voice only a touch bitter, "some guys get used to beautiful women, fast cars, adoring fans, too much money, pots of caviar, me..." I spread my arms wide and then simply shrugged. Norman smiled. Jeeter laughed out loud.

At that point Boll and Larry came out of the kitchen. The owner/chef looked as proud as a human being can look. Whatever brand of banana oil Boll used on him, I had to give her credit—he appeared to be as distracted as a man possibly could.

As the agent took her seat once more, Larry begged off, admitting he had spent too much time away from his unusually large morning crowd. Somewhat embarrassed over the fact he wanted to spread himself around and meet all the celebrities he could, we good-naturedly laughed at him a bit, then wished him happy hunting and sent him on his way.

"One of those has-to-know-everything types," Norman half-asked, half-stated. Jeeter backed up his assessment, adding that Larry was just one of those harmless characters of which every town has at least one. Boll sided with the sheriff, finishing:

"Besides, anyone who makes as good a waffle as Larry does should be cut a certain amount of slack."

"Why, Ms. Boll," I answered with a fair degree of honest astonishment in my voice, "what a kind and generous comment. Who wrote it for you?"

"Bite me, dickwad," she snarled.

"Ohhhhh, thanks for the kind offer, but I don't dare," I answered innocently. "At my age I have to take care of my teeth."

I truly thought I was being amusing. Evidently Boll didn't agree with my assessment. Her hand shot across the table, her fingers closing around my tie before I could back away. Helplessly, for lack of a better word, I stared at her unblinking, my eyes wide and my mouth open as she spat:

"Get off my goddamned back, you little maggot or, useful of

not, I will put you through a wall." Quietly sipping his coffee, Norman simply added:

"She can do it, too. I'd listen, Carl."

"Yeah," added Jeeter, smiling himself, "a man who slaps a dog shouldn't be surprised when one bites him. You know what your problem is, Kolchak, you just don't know how to act around pretty girls."

Boll released me at that point and I went crashing backward against my chair, nearly toppling over against the person behind me in my haste to put some distance between the two of us. I noticed both Norman and Boll giving Jeeter a look out of the corner of their eyes. They were very different looks, and the sheriff ignored them both, spearing hash browns and sausages as if he didn't have a care in the world.

He actually may not have had any major cares at that moment, either, but as if the way of things, the mere fact he was at peace for the moment, fate simply had to bring something his way. Just as the four of us were about to get back to our discussion, the front door opened with a bang. Two of the sheriff's deputies entered—both agitated, one standing firm, the other heading for our table. As he came close, he threw Jeeter a hurried salute, then bent low to whisper:

"Will, trouble at the Holister place." Tension immediately flared around the table. As all eyes locked on the deputy, the sheriff asked:

"Is the word 'trouble' something you care to give a bit more definition?" When the lawman nodded questioningly toward the rest of us, Jeeter made a "never mind them" kind of hand motion, urging the deputy to continue. Coming closer to the table, the man said:

"Word just came in at the station--somebody torched the farm. It's in flames, and threatening to spread." ●

CHAPTER TWENTY-SIX

One thing about reporters, they know how to jump on each other's action. Seeing me leave behind the sheriff, practically everyone else in Larry's place jumped up, threw cash on their tables and headed outside to follow along. Those stuck with expense accounts left aide's behind with the company credit card as they hurried to the door. To keep the sheriff from looking as if he was playing favorites too heavily, I traveled with Norman and Boll while the sheriff simply got into the cruiser his deputies had waiting.

Fire crews were called in from six neighboring townships and villages. It hadn't been raining or snowing much yet that season, and most everything around was unseasonably dry. The main house and the barns had gone up instantly as planned by whoever the local firebug was, but so had everything else in sight. Fences, trees, grass blazed, telephone wires melted and their poles burned--the Holister place was lost, a complete and utter inferno by the time we arrived.

The firetrucks already on the scene weren't trying to save anything of the farm. It was far too late for that. Their job was to fight a holding action, keeping the blaze from spreading to any of the neighboring farms or the town. Cameras clicked by the dozens all around us. As video crews arrived, an onslaught of microphones chased after Jeeter, demanding answers, even as he tried to get some for himself. As the sheriff struggled to maintain his composure in the face of the horde, Norman, Boll and myself hung back, taking shelter from prying ears across the road and behind the neighbor's fence. All of us continued to watch the fire, of course, even as we tried to make sense of it.

"This is no surprise," said Boll. "Is it?"

"Not really," agreed Norman. "We suspected human intervention in the form of the killer--not a free-range evil, but something created. Add that to Carl being 'Deed and Beed' ..."

"Add that to me being what?"

"D&B," the agent answered me, "Deed and Beed, drugged and bugged." I nodded as he turned back to Boll, telling her, "No, really isn't anything unexpected about this fire. Somebody is wanting all their tracks covered."

"Wait a minute," I threw out. "Something just hit me. That warning you sent me. You didn't just come up with any of this. You knew! You knew something was off around here."

"It's our job to investigate these kinds of incidents," Norman said calmly. "Remember? The fact we stumble across you once in a while doesn't mean we're following you."

"Fine," I snapped. "So your eight steps ahead of me. You were here first. Then why aren't you helping me here? Why am I getting invaded and drugged and ..."

And then it hit me. As the answer formed in my head, I could see in Norman's eyes that I was right. Still needing to hear it, though, I said:

"Of course, of course you knew. You sent me the note to key me up, getting me watching for everything and anything. But, you didn't move in until something happened to me. You sons of bitches, you set me up. Left me to take the fire of whatever was coming while you sat safe and comfy in your tree to watch and see what happened."

"Why all the surprise, Carl," asked Boll, enjoying herself as she did. "We're the FBI, little man. We're not here to help you. Much as your big fish ego likes to make everything about you, yours is a very small pond, one we can step over without too much trouble, and apparently without you even noticing."

I could feel my face turning red. I had been wandering around behind them all morning, trusting them, feeling as if suddenly I was safe and secure, free from harm in the sheltering arms of my government. All I could think was, whoever had drugged me the night before had certainly sprung for the good stuff. I felt like a fool, like a rank amateur. I was a fish in a pond, all right, apparently one willing to bite on the first lure that broke the water.

"Well, notice this," I told her, flipping her the one-finger salute as I turned and walked away from the pair of them. Norman, in his carefully modulated, always professionally courteous voice, reminded me that I hadn't brought my own car and that it was more than a few miles back to town. I didn't answer.

Did I like the idea of walking all the way back to town--of

course not. Did I think I was going to prove anything to anyone? Not really. Any assumptions I could confirm for people by such a stunt I had most likely confirmed for them ages ago with some other form of rash and ill-planned behavior. Still, I didn't care. This was a matter of pride. I had no idea how I was going to pay back the two FBI agents for their treatment of me, or exactly what it was I was paying them back for, but breathing the air of the righteous, I stormed off anyway, determined in the best tradition of knuckle-headed behavior to "show them a thing or two."

By the time I made the main road I was regretting my show of righteous indignation. A mile down the road I was regretting it severely. I'd created my scene back near a roaring fire. It was a lot easier to think about storming off when I was warm. But the further I got from the Holister place, the colder I was getting. Not only was I away from the fire, but there was nothing around me on the open road--nothing to stop the mounting wind from tearing through my bones, chilling me to the point of collapse.

At least, I told myself, I still had my overcoat, and I whispered a short prayer of thanks to God for it. On that lonely, freezing road, I didn't care if the guy who'd owned it before me was the most hated guy in town or not. Hell, as my ears started tingling, frost settling into their grooves, I didn't care if he was the most hated guy on the planet.

More than just the fact it was keeping me warm, however, it was the fact that LuAnn had picked it out for me. I'd only managed to spend a short amount of time with her so far, but it had been the only enjoyable moments I'd spent since I'd left California. As that thought rolled down the center of my mind, whispers from several of the side alleys asked me just how many enjoyable moments I'd had before I left.

Some people might have grown depressed at that moment, moaning over how empty their life had been up until that point. Not me. I've lived through enough bad times that I don't see the sense in hanging onto any of them. Remembering the past and learning from it is one thing. Keeping it around to cry over is for chumps. And, while I'm not saying I've never played the role of the chump in my time, I try not to rehearse for it every minute of the day like some people.

As I continued my miserable forced march back to town, plenty of vehicles continued to race along the other side of the road, every reporter, anchorman and second string article writer in the area headed out to the fire. No one seemed interested in heading into Gore, of course, which meant the old Kolchak luck was still batting in the high numbers. I kept hoping that a bus, or car service driver, or even a truck with a load bed full of chickens I could sit with, would come along. But Carl, the depressing voice from the back of my mind whispered, if there was anything like that headed into town, they probably stopped at the Holister place to see what all the commotion was about.

I didn't answer myself. I sounded too right to argue with. And for at least the first hour or so of my walk, that's the way it was until a sedan eased its way around me, then slowed, stopped, and began to back up. The driver maneuvered around me with a careful ease, stopping parallel to me as if such a maneuver on a dirt road was the simplest thing in the world. As the passenger side window came down, a male voice I didn't recognize said:

"Can't imagine why you'd be walking in this weather, Mr. Kolchak, but if you've had enough of the morning air for the moment, I'd be happy to give you a ride into town."

Not worrying about who it was or how they knew my name, I jumped at the chance to stop freezing and clambered inside as quickly as my stiffening joints would allow. I figured, I was in the middle of nowhere, if it was someone who wanted me dead they could just shoot me and leave me on the side of the road.

As I shut the door I took several deep breaths of the toasty air inside the car. My ears started burning almost instantly from the change in temperature. I took off my hat and rubbed the top of my head, my scalp tingling instantly as it sighed in relief along with the rest of my body. The driver, after making certain I was all inside, started up again and headed for Gore at a nice clip. I pushed myself into the quite comfortable passenger bucket seat and thanked God for the Samaritan he had sent me even more so than I did earlier for my coat.

As we started down the road again, I remembered the rules and I shoved myself into my side of the car's legally mandated shoulder harness and seat belt. Don't get me wrong; I'm not one of these guys who snarls over every move the government makes, but I do think passing out tickets to people who don't want to be strapped down is a bit obnoxious. The things have jammed and trapped more than one person inside a burning vehicle.

I do get testy over air bags, however. The things have killed over one hundred of the people they were supposed to be saving—mostly small women and children--as they exploded out of their hiding places, and yet the government still refuses to allow people to disconnect them. Their answer, just make anyone who isn't tough enough to survive being smacked in the face and chest with incredible force sit in the back. If you don't, we'll give you another ticket. But, that's the level of quality thinking you get in Washington.

Once I was all buckled in, safe and secure, I turned to my savior and thanked him for stopping. Then, my memory thawing out a bit, I asked:

"You have to forgive me, but I have to admit I don't recognize you. But, you called me by name. Have we met since I arrived, or... well..." The man chuckled good-naturedly, and waved my embarrassment off with a casual gesture, explaining:

"No, no sir. We haven't met. But, this is a small town and as you might suspect, everyone knows everyone else's business around here. You can't buy a coat like the one you did and not have everyone treating it like news on a par with the election of a new Pope. Or even that which has been going on here in our little back yard which has the entire nation's attention glued to us these days."

"Oh, man--this coat," I groaned. "I'm telling you, it's a wonderful coat, but you're right. Everyone knows it. And they all seem to have hated the guy who owned it before me." The driver nodded in agreement with my statement. Finally curious enough to want to know, I asked:

"So, who was the baby-killer who owned this thing before me, anyway?"

"Oh, my," the driver answered, laughing gently, "why that was my coat." ●

CHAPTER TWENTY-SEVEN

"My apologies, Mr. Kolchak," my host offered, chuckling to himself with amusement. "I couldn't help having that little bit of fun. Do forgive me."

"What am I forgiving you for, exactly," I asked, trying to remember exactly how breathing worked and to put the information into use.

"My name is Carmine Esposito. I'm the president of Haberton College. I'm afraid I made quite a few enemies locally when I was brought in to put the school back on its feet years ago."

Esposito proved to be a quite cultured and dignified man. A touch shorter than me, most likely in his sixties, gray hair, neatly trimmed moustache and beard, thin to the point where he actually looked somewhat dehydrated, he quickly proved to be a witty conversationalist— one who gave me his entire story quite concisely.

Haberton had been ready to close its doors. The school's executives had not paid attention to its standing in years— decades, really—and their accreditation was on the line. Esposito had come in and cleaned house. Professors not teaching up to his efficient standards were sacked, whole departments were ruthlessly emptied. Students unable to handle the tough new workload were dismissed as well.

He had thrown out the far too scattered liberal arts approach to learning of the past and greatly narrowed the school's focus, streamlining its programs to help Haberton hold its own in the modern world. Now it turned out many of the nation's top electronics scholars for the video and computer marketplaces.

"You could say I tore the ivy down off the walls and dusted the place off. I made a lot of people mad, but they were the kind of folks you meet everywhere-people who couldn't understand that if the incompetent and the lazy didn't lose their jobs, then everyone was going to lose their jobs."

"People are like that," I said, agreeing with him. LuAnn had told me something of the school's history, and had nothing but praise for Esposito.

"Yes, they are. They want their cake, they want to eat it, and then they want more cake for dessert. But, ranting about that kind of thing serves no purpose. We old men have to watch ourselves, or we'll fly off the handle every chance we get."

Well, I thought, at least I knew why everyone in Gore had such a dislike for the man. No one likes an outsider who comes in and fires a bunch of locals, even if they are the problem that's dragging not only themselves, but everyone else down as well. As if he were reading my mind, Esposito added:

"I've been down here nearly twenty years now; you'd think people could let a thing go... auk, there I go again. Quick, Mr. Kolchak, tell me about yourself and your work before I drift off into senility before your very eyes."

I gave my host the fifty cent tour of my past, skimming over such things as mummies and hell hounds. To my surprise, as with Larry, my fame had preceded me with Esposito. He turned out to be a touch more familiar with my career than I would have imagined. When I said so, he responded:

"You're quite blunt, Mr. Kolchak. I like that. Cutting to the heart of things gets results. As I said earlier, it's a very small town you're in. An outsider starts escorting one of our local ladies to dinner on a regular basis... people talk, you know."

I really had been in Hollywood too long, I thought. It was one thing to watch Andy Griffith reruns, it was another to spend a week in Mayberry itself. As I pulled at my collar, feeling like a schoolboy caught with the teacher's guide to that week's history test in my back pocket, we pulled into the Gore business district. Esposito slowed accordingly, finishing his thought by saying:

"Ms. Hildebergen is well thought of at Haberton. And, in a college town in the age of the Internet, it really didn't take long before her new beau was the talk of the campus." Esposito smiled wryly, asking me:

"And now, you must forgive me, but I must avail myself of this opportunity. Tell me, did you really kill a vampire, Mr. Kolchak?"

I don't know why, but for some reason I never felt more embarrassed in all my life. It was if my grandfather was asking me the question. Before I could say anything one way or the other, the president of Haberton let me off the hook, telling me that I could wait until later to answer the question. He seemed honestly interested in hearing me speak on the supernatural, and I began to wonder if he was talking about us simply continuing our conversation, or having me stand up in from of an auditorium filled with students.

"I have to head out to the campus right now, and unless you'd like a tour of Haberton, which I would have to delegate to the first warm body I found, I'm afraid, if you just tell me where I can drop you off..."

We were close enough to the 1,2,3! that I told him I could get out where we were. I told him that not only had he done more than enough for me, but that after the number of freezing miles he had spared me, a few minutes of chilly reminder on exactly how dangerous ego can be might be just the thing I needed. He laughed with an innocence that told me he might have done the same kind of foolish thing himself somewhere in the past. Merely nodding knowingly at me, he then extended an offer of cigars and brandy some night before I returned to the coast. Handing me his business card so I might call him if I had the chance, he thanked me for my company as if I had done him the favor, and then drove off in what I assumed was the direction of Haberton.

I hoofed it the few blocks to my motel and headed straight for my room. I found the bed made, the bathroom straighten, but no evidence of any other entry outside of the maid. Of course, I hadn't seen any evidence of anyone else coming or going until Norman showed me the various listening devices strewn about the room, either.

Shrugging off Carmine Esposito's old coat, throwing my old hat on top of it, I immediately headed for my laptop to get to work. Switching it on, I watched it warm up, looking for some tell-tale evidence it had been tampered with. Nothing seemed different, all my files were in place, every "i" still dotted, every "t" still crossed.

Giving up on paranoia, I got down to cranking out more news for an information-starved public. I did a piece on the sheriff and the coroner burning the crime scenes to protect the public from possible infection. While I was writing, I downloaded the photos I had taken of those actions from my camera and emailed them to Vincenzo. Oddly enough, it was thinking of my faithful Brooklyn-born tortoise that lead me to the answer that had been sitting before me the entire time. ●

CHAPTER TWENTY-EIGHT

As I was emailing the article off to the *Dispatch* offices, I started pondering the implications of the fire at the Holister place. We had torched the previous two crime scenes to rid them of all traces of the nightmarish plant-things growing there. Although we had discussed the necessity of doing something to the massive potential breeding grounds at crime scene #3, it's one thing to pour some gasoline on a piece of pavement and light it, it's another to burn buildings to the ground.

It entered my mind then that one of the things that kept me sharp was Vincenzo's constant nagging for his reporters to get all the facts, to assume nothing, to make no leaps of faith simply because it was convenient. But, even looking at the new fire through his eyes, it seemed evident that the cause had to be arson, and the reason had to be involvement in the murders.

I wouldn't have dared present the idea from my dreams to Vincenzo as any kind of proof. Even I wouldn't have thought I had enough to go on simply because I'd put two and two together in a drunken dream. But, dreams are where we work out the problems of the waking world, and when Boll had mentioned "hybrids," I knew I was on the right track.

So, I wondered, just who would be making hybrid monsters? It had to be a someone. Plants and animals don't just start mating on their own. Be it a magician or a scientist, someone was snipping together bits and pieces to generate monsters. It simply had to be.

Vincenzo looking over my shoulder, all the basic questions tumbled out, begging to be answered: who, what, when, where, why? "Who?" I had no idea. "What?" was putting monsters together; "When?" was recently; "Where" was somewhere in the area. And then

"Why?" How the hell to answer that one?

As if to prove he was the boss, my cell phone rang then, with Vincenzo on the other end. He complimented me on what I had just sent him, on the fine job I'd been doing. He asked what else was coming. I told him. All of it. I gave him everything that had happened that I hadn't already sent along in the form of news.

To say he was not happy that monsters were rearing their ugly heads again was the understatement of the year. And then, just as he began to make it clear how unhappy he was to hear such things, the link I had been looking for fell out of the sky and into my head. Conscious of the listening devices all around me, I told my happily barking turtle to hold on while I got my hat and coat on. I lied that if I had to listen to him, I was going to do it with coffee to brace me.

Once outside, not trusting my cell phone not to be bugged by the FBI, I walked several blocks, purposely passing by the first two pay phones I saw until I found another. If those wanting to listen in on my conversations were as thorough as they seemed, I imagined they might go after the public phones as well. Fishing some change out of my pocket, I made a collect call to the *Dispatch*, and then filled Vincenzo in on the FBI connection, on the load of listening devices they had found in my room, and on everything else I hadn't said inside because I hadn't wanted inquiring minds to know.

"Listen to me, Tony, something just hit me that's going to tear this whole thing open."

"Kolchak," he groaned, "for the love of St. Peter, why do you have to do these things to me?"

"Tony, you don't understand. Think—the FBI's here because they want to know what's going on. Who built this thing? And why? But there's another 'why' question. 'Why' did they put it to use now? As a test--I don't think so. Why test it on some guy in the middle of no where? A guy who would be missed, that would attract national attention? That doesn't make any sense."

"What's your point, Carl?"

"What if it wasn't a random guy in the middle of nowhere? What if Wendel Halford was specifically targeted? What if someone wanted him dead and used this thing that just grows, kills, then disappears?"

"And why would someone with this super weapon want to kill a guy who made yogurt for a living?"

"What if the guy who made yogurt for a living had the one thing you wanted, Tony? What if you were in possession of this super weapon, as you call it, and you were in love with his wife?"

I could tell by the way my faithful turtle had stopped breathing for a moment that I had hit a nerve. As fast as I could, I told him of Mark Kenny and Veronica Halford. He was breathing again in seconds, happy enough to admit knowing me to strangers.

"This sounds good, Carl," he admitted, the tone in his voice a touch distracted. It was easy enough to figure out where his mind was. It also came roaring back quickly enough to make speculation moot. Barking into the phone, he shouted:

"Now you listen to me, Carl, I want the FBI on the record on this. I want you to slide this one home smooth. Don't you blow this, you hear me, Kolchak? You get this sheriff or these agents or the goddamned Shadow, for all I care, and you get this guy into somebody's custody and you be the first one to talk to him. But, don't you do anything stupid. Don't you ..."

I let him rant for a while, knowing he only did it out of love. Then, finally letting him know I needed to get moving, he got serious enough to remind me to be careful and to take care of myself. After that I thanked him for his concern then killed the connection so I could get on the road. Hurrying back to the 1,2,3! parking lot, I slid into my rental and fired it up.

Once on the road I headed straight for the sheriff's office. Vincenzo had been right about getting some help for approaching Kenny. If I was right, at the very least the guy had access to super-monsters and wasn't afraid to sic them on his enemies. I found Jeeter in his office behind closed doors with Campbell. The place was jammed with a sea of media, of whom I was just another part of the flotsam. Dialing in the sheriff's private number which he'd given me earlier, I got an earful from him, picking up where Vincenzo had left off.

After explaining why I'd left so abruptly from Holister's, I told him of what I'd pieced together. He agreed with me that there was something at the least suspicious about Kenny and the widow Halford. The local grapevine had been commenting on her lack of proper upset. It was true that the two of them could just be tacky, but putting the lights to Kenny's eyes was not only the first positive, but offensive thing that had been suggested to Jeeter since the entire case had begun. Apparently tired of playing a defensive action, as he put it:

"It'd be nice to do a little pushin' for once, instead of just pushin' back."

"I agree," I said, smiling to myself. Then, starting to warm to the upcoming, I asked, "so, how do we handle this?"

Jeeter's answer was to put his hat on Campbell's head and to push the deputy out into the media frenzy while he went out the back door and joined me in the sheriff's department parking lot. He suggested we take his cruiser. Knowing it was certain to have more weapons than my ugliest-green-hatchback in the world, I agreed.

Since there was no other parking, he told me to pull my car into his spot. After that, we were on our way and frankly feeling fairly good about things for once. We had a plan, one that just might help put an end to the horror that had three states in a major panic, or at least start the process. We were, as we pulled out of the lot and onto the main road, confident that finally we were one step ahead of the competition.

Someday I'm going to make one of those speeches about keeping my ego in check, and I'm actually going to listen to it. ●

CHAPTER TWENTY-NINE

The sheriff was betting Kenny was on campus rather than at home. He still had one of his men put a call into the professor's residence, just in case. All they reported was an obnoxious answering machine message that went on too long with one of the Eagles' worse songs as background noise. As we neared the college, Jeeter commented that something like that message alone should have tipped folks off to Kenny having criminal tendencies.

I told Jetter that I didn't know enough about the Eagles' music to have an opinion. He asked if this was the first time I'd ever admitted such a thing and then started laughing. I refused to dignify his unwarranted attack with an answer.

As we pulled onto the Haberton campus, I was impressed with the look of the place. The university had been built on the outskirts of town so that as it grew it would have no trouble expanding. Even though the place was only some seventy, eighty years old, it possessed the solid, mature aura of a much more ancient and prestigious institution. Esposito might have dragged the place into efficient profitability, but he hadn't done so at the expense of its dignity, despite what he might have said about "tearing down the ivy" as soon as he got there. I caught myself writing cover copy for one of the school's brochures in my head, and wondered if I would be so enthusiastic about the place if I wasn't, as the place's president had put it, escorting one of its "local young ladies" to dinner on a regular basis.

I also took the moment to marvel at how truly fortunate I'd been on this story. The Carl Kolchak luck is usually a thing tied up in its owner being bounced from one closed door to the next. Having the local law enforcers not only treating me civilly, but taking me into their confidences and looking to me for advice and the such--well, it was just a nice change of pace. One I was hoping might last longer than just however much time I had left in Gore.

"If I'm not bein' too forward," said Jeeter as he pulled into a parking spot close to the administrating building, "why don't we give your Ms. Hildebergen a try? Havin' someone on our side who knows the lay of the land might just get us quicker results."

I agreed with him, but told him I was embarrassed to admit that I didn't know where to find LuAnn on campus. He surprised me by answering that he did. As he explained:

"When she first moved in down here, there was more than one of us made our play for her. She was friendly enough, didn't hurt anyone's feelin', not much, anyway... but outside of a few dates, she really didn't take much of a shine to anyone." He allowed the thought to hang in the air until we were both out of the cruiser. Then, just as we pulled together on the sidewalk, he allowed a playful smile to cross his face as he casually added:

"That is, before a certain big city reporter hit town and somehow just swept her off her feet."

If I thought I'd felt a bit of embarrassment at not knowing where LuAnn's office was, I found myself drowning in a barrel of the stuff after that. I caught a look in Jeeter's eye that made me wonder if he'd made a pass at her himself. He cleared that one up for me, saying:

"And if you're thinkin' I was one of the young fools wastin' his money and time trying to impress her, you'd be wrong. I've seen myself in a mirror, you know, and I do remember how far back it was when my birthdays started. No--I found out where her office was because after a while the only way I could find Campbell, and a couple other of my sorry knuckleheads, was to drop in on her. Seems their radios and cell phones just stopped workin' whenever they hit campus."

"She is quite a woman," I answered.

"Yeah, but she ain't why we're here, so let's get to it and see if we can put a cork in this thing."

We made a straight line for LuAnn's corner of Haberton, the sheriff in the lead mainly because he knew the way. As we first entered, she seemed pleased to see us. Then, something in either Jeeter's face or mine gave away the fact that we weren't there on a social call. We explained what we were after. When we told her we needed to find Mark Kenny's office, or more importantly, Kenny himself, she asked:

"Why? What's he done? Is he involved with what's been going

on? What..." Jeeter held up his hand, palm toward LuAnn, making a friendly, but definite gesture for her to stop talking. As she slowed down into quiet, he told her:

"Ms. Hildebergen, since this is a sensitive matter, and one we're only just beginnin' to pull together, I really can't answer any of your questions. It's just the legal niceties and all, you understand." He let his eyes flicker in my direction for a moment, then linked them back to hers as he added:

"I'm certain there's someone around here who'll fill you in later on all you want to know. Someone not bound by the law to keep his fat yap shut like I am. You understand, don't you, ma'am?"

LuAnn nodded tensely. She, like everyone else in the area, was concerned over what had been happening of late. People get like that when they know a super-powered killing machine that tears people, cows, horses and police cars apart like tissue paper, one that doesn't leave tracks, can't be heard, and as of the attack on I-95, can't be stopped by bullets, either, is on the loose.

Neither of us blamed her for wanting to know what was going on. We just couldn't tell her right then. She knew Jeeter was telling her the truth, however, and didn't give him a hard time about it. After he thanked her for that, she said:

"Mark's office is in the back wing, the nice section. That's where all the R&D fellowshipers have their offices."

"'R&D fellowshipers'...?"

"Sorry, sheriff," LuAnn said in response. "Research and development. Kenny is one of the faculty scientists, he doesn't really teach all that much; that's left up to graduate assistants. He's a rainmaker, here to develop new finds, bring the college the kind of notoriety it needs to pull in new grants and the such."

We both nodded as she talked. Neither of us had possessed much of an idea of what Kenny did at Haberton. Now we knew. He was a scientist, working on developing new things. It was still all circumstantial, but more and more of our bits and pieces were falling into place every second. Jeeter and I simply traded glances. We could each tell the other was thinking the same thing. As we turned our attention back to LuAnn, she said:

"No one is allowed in that area without authorization. Of course, sheriff, you could get inside on your own authority, but it would take a moment, and Kenny might be alerted. If you give me just a minute, I'll take you there. If I'm leading the way, we can probably just walk right in."

Jeeter agreed. LuAnn's only duty was to call in to Esposito. She apparently had to bring him a set of reports he'd been expecting, and she said she just wanted to check and see if he was in before heading over. As we left, she explained she could have just walked the reports over and dropped them off at his receptionist's desk. But, having done things this way, word would be left that she was coming and no one would give her or anyone with her a second glance.

I tend to trust that people know more about their own workplace than I do. Apparently Jeeter did as well, for neither of us said anything. We simply fell in line behind LuAnn and allowed her to lead us off toward the new wing. It was somewhat of a hike, but after about twenty minutes of going down stairs, outside, past several buildings, and then finally into one at the very edge of the campus and up several more flights of stairs we finally made it to the new wing.

"No wonder you're in such good shape," I said, feeling a bit winded from the walk. "You have to make this trip very many times a day?"

LuAnn laughed lightly, and Jeeter smiled. She was just about to make an answer when a noise in the distance caught our attention. It was low, and somewhat muffled, but I was fairly certain I knew what had made it. From the way Jeeter sprang forward, his left hand unconsciously clawing at his holster, dragging his sidearm out and up to the ready, I figured he was dead certain of what he'd heard.

We ran down the corridor in the direction of the sound. By the time we arrived at the end of the hallway, there was no mistaking in which direction we should turn. A crowd had begun to gather in front of one of the doors halfway down the side hall going left. We went that way, afraid we knew exactly what we were going to find.

"Stand aside, please."

Jeeter had to tell no one twice. His official voice was a dark and powerful thing that parted the crowd before any of them saw his badge or uniform or the weapon in his hand. I followed closely on his heels, LuAnn right behind me. As we came up to the door, we found the name "Professor Mark Kenny" on a plaque next to it. Jeeter told everyone to stand back and then opened the door. He went in prepared, taunt and ready for anything. After only a small handful of seconds, however, his body relaxed.

As he slid his weapon back into his holster, I peeked inside around the door jam. Mark Kenny was in his office waiting for us, all right. But he wouldn't be answering any of our questions. Not with his brains blown out across the wall behind him. ●

CHAPTER THIRTY

"You know, Carl," Jeeter said to me as he and his men were finishing up their preliminary investigation there in Kenny's office, "you sure do have a knack for bein' on my coattails when the shit comes down."

"Well now, sheriff, I'm not sure if you're telling me something here or not," I said, more than a little attitude spilling over into my tone. As soon as I said the words, however, I immediately back-pedaled, saying, "Strike that, Will. I apologize. I think I'm still feeling a bit abused from this morning when my little FBI buddies started dropping crap on me."

Jeeter nodded sympathetically, as if just the mention of the FBI was enough to generate sympathy for anyone. Taking every granule of pity I could get, the kind coming from others so much more refreshing that the self-generated kind, I admitted:

"I guess hearing anything that reminded me I'm 'only' a reporter hits a sensitive area right now."

"Don't sweat the small stuff, Carl," the sheriff answered. He was looking a bit tired, but also fairly well pleased with himself. And, I thought, why shouldn't he be? For all intents and purposes, he had just put the lid on both his case and my story.

Pulling out his ever-present flask, Wiffalon also made a comment about having seen all he needed to of me for a while, and then took a slug while I chuckled. The three of us had become something of a team, and they had both just been playing with me the way guys do. I threw some crap back at them at that point, letting them know I was as simian as the next guy, and we all laughed the nervous laughter of the greatly relieved. We all also took our well-deserve swigs from Wiffalon's flask.

And really, why shouldn't we? As best we could tell, it was all over. There would be no more killings. No more slaughters. Mark Kenny had tied everything up for us in one neat little bundle, and we were all grateful, to say the least.

"Still hard to believe just one normal guy could have caused all the damage he did," said Campbell. "At least, for the reason he did."

Standing in the doorway to Kenny's office, the deputy had been called in to keep the crowd back while Jeeter and Wiffalon conducted their investigation. I was allowed to stay inside the office because, frankly, both men had really stopped thinking of me as a reporter, and more like one of the guys. Reporters to them were the hordes of arrogant creeps that were outside in the streets of Gore making a nightmare of their town.

Both had found their offices inundated with requests for copies of crime scene photos, for interviews, permissions to cross police lines, everything to be exclusive, everything to be done immediately, at the media's convenience, all of it coming with a feeling that it was deserved, that those making the requests could have made demands instead, but that they were just being nice. Gore was not a town that gave over much consideration to capped teeth and three piece suits.

Finally, I thought, my wardrobe and life style are paying off.

Of course, their case being solved meant my business in Gore was pretty much done. Oh, I figured I could squeeze an extra week out of the story--today's news would take two to three days to filter, easily. Back-up interviews could get me a few more extensions, but sooner or later, I realized, I was going to have to go back to Hollywood. Away from Virginia. Away from old man winter.

Away from LuAnn.

"So, Carl--did you think it would be this easy?"

"No, Tom," I answered the coroner, "I have to admit I thought we were in for a much rougher time of things."

"You and me both, amigo," added Jeeter. "You and goddamned me, both."

Relief seemed to be the key ingredient in the make-up of both men's faces. Although none of us had said anything, there was no doubting both of them had felt as I did, that this whole affair would have to end in fire and blood, with some kind of hell beast slaughtering everything in sight. But, for once I was going to get off easy. For once no monster—at least, not on camera, as it were. And all

I had to do was say "goodbye" to a woman whom every second was making me feel like all I wanted in life was to be able to come through the door at the end of the day and shout, "honey, I'm home," and have someone there to hear it. Someone like her. Exactly like her.

"Why so glum, Carl," asked Wiffalon. I gave him a shrug, as if I wasn't certain, but the sheriff helped me out by saying:

"Catch a clue; ol' Kolchak here, he's all in love--ain't ya?"

"Give me a break," I said quietly. I think he'd been expecting a bit of my usual sarcasm. It seemed clear from the way he suddenly looked embarrassed that he had thought he was exaggerating the situation. I didn't blame him. Until he said the words out loud, I hadn't even admitted the idea of it to myself--not completely. As I just stared, too tongue-tied and embarrassed myself to say anything in return, Jeeter hung his head a bit, making us look like Spanky and Alfalfa being sent to the principal's office. Finally, he said:

"Sorry, Carl--I didn't know it was really that serious. I thought I was just funnin' with ya."

"It's all right. I'm a little surprised myself."

The three of us started grinning like loons then as it became clear that I actually was crazy about Gore's Ms. Hildebergen. The two of them razzed me for a little about it, but finally we figured we should finish up what we were doing and let the college get back to being a college and not a crime scene. Deciding to get that accomplished as quickly as possible, the sheriff went out into the hall to explain things to the Haberton administration while I helped Wiffalon bag what was left of Kenny.

Digging into his valise, the coroner pulled out two sets of throw-away rubber gloves. As we put them on, he asked:

"So Carl, tell me--how's all this sit with you?" When I asked him what he meant, he explained, "You've seen everything Jeeter and I have. You buying the package or what?"

"Are you saying you're not?"

"I don't know. Maybe I just read too many mysteries. I just keep looking at what we have and it feels like maybe this was all a bit too convenient." Since we were stuffing a human body inside a bag at that moment, I wasn't exactly certain where the convenience was, but I was as willing to swipe at a dangling threat as much as the next feline. Holding the body bag open, and as far from myself as possible as Wiffalon crammed Kenny's remains inside, we discussed his idea.

Kenny had been more than a simple teaching professor. He'd also been one of the college's top research scientists. His suicide letter spelled out that my hunch had been right. He had been crazy for Veronica Halford, and had murdered her husband. As his letter explained, my other gut instinct had been correct as well. Being a bio-chemist, he had tinkered together a form of plant life which had done the job for him.

He wasn't expecting us to believe he had created this killing machine simply because he wanted to kill someone. No, according to his letter, the dirty little secret around Haberton was that the supposed liberal college was doing research and development for the military. The thing Kenny had used to kill Wendel Halford was the result of years of work, not all of it his.

Somehow, he and his team had crossed the building blocks of certain mammals with certain plants and come up with a fast growing hybrid which could be introduced into an environment just by tossing it onto a patch of open ground. He had pieced together Wendel's schedule talking to Veronica, and timed his "planting" of his assassin to coincide with his victim's smoke break. It had worked like a charm.

But, what he hadn't counted on was that he didn't know everything about the weapon they'd created. The problem with their super soldier was that it couldn't be trained to recognize good guys from bad guys. Or to stop killing. Kenny had believed the things dried up and disintegrated after a short period of life, and he'd been correct. But, after the second killing he'd gone back into the files and found out that while the things did collapse after a short period, they didn't die. They simply went dormant the way plants do, and then grew again. They did not grow as fast, which accounted for the length of time between killings, but they grew stronger. And, as we had discovered, they left behind blood-drinking spores.

"I mean," Wiffalon said as he tugged the body bag's zipper closed, "Kenny let's this thing loose, then he sneaks out to the Holister place and burns it down. Then he goes across the state to lure this thing to him out on a dark stretch of I-95 ..."

"And, I'll point out," I interjected, "he did not explain how he managed that trick."

"No, he didn't, but while he was putting his critter down, which he also didn't explain, he ends up attracting the state police's attention, and lets his killer carrot take them out before he finishes it off once and for all."

"It is a bit much ..."

"I don't know," the coroner huffed, "it does all make sense. I mean, if we're going to believe plants and animals can have their DNA intermixed... maybe we can believe the rest of it."

He did have a point. Men about to blow their brains out really can't be held accountable if they leave a few details out of their suicide note. Besides, Kenny didn't want his creature unleashed on the world. Even by the good guys. He claimed that he destroyed all his notes, everything he could about how to create his monsters. There would be an investigation, of course, and the college and the military would provide headlines for some time, but for all intents and purposes, the countryside was safe. The killer was gone. Everything was over.

When Wiffalon's man came, the two of them loaded Kenny onto a small portable gurney the assistant had brought. Just as they were leaving, the junior coroner asked about Kenny's blood on the wall. Wiffalon said he'd gathered enough to do his work, yelled at the young man to do as he was told, then took a final slug from his flask and disappeared out the door.

As I stood there in Kenny's office, I suddenly realized I was still wearing my throw-away gloves. Wiffalon had peeled his off and tossed them inside the body bag. Being busy talking, I hadn't realized I should've done the same. Peeling them off, I thought about throwing them in the wastebasket, but that seemed tacky. Then, as the door began to open I panicked and shoved them inside my coat pocket. I instantly felt foolish, but then I thought, what the hell, I was going to get rid of the coat anyway, so who cared?

Turning my attention back to the door, I found Campbell leaning in to tell me the sheriff wanted the room sealed. Because of my nonsense with the bloody gloves, I found myself staring at more of Kenny's blood, the blood mixed with his brains that was smeared against the wall behind his desk. As the deputy said my name again, I suddenly realized what it was that had caught my attention in all that scarlet. I apologized for day-dreaming, then hustled out of the office.

As quickly as I could, I made my way to the lower levels—the basement levels. On our way in, Jeeter and I had wondered if we should go after Kenny in his office or in the research center. We had decided to let LuAnn decide, figuring she would know where he was. She had.

But, staring at the inside of Kenny's skull smeared across the wall, I had suddenly realized that wasn't the only mess he had left there at Haberton. His section of the research center would have to be in a shambles. Did he burn files, shred them, just dump them in the wastebasket? And his computer—did he merely delete files, or did he remember that his hard drive would have to be purged? Did he even know how many copies there were of his work?

It hadn't been two hours since Kenny had taken the easy way out. That meant it was possible the lab might not have been cleared out by either the university or the Pentagon's spin police. I had no idea what I might be able to find there, but I was determined if there was anything to find there, I was going to be the newshound who found it first. Ol' Freddie Nietzsche once said that nobody knew what news was important until a hundred years had passed. Not having that long to wait, I figured I'd get down there and see what I could discover right away.

And, all things considered, it was probably the single most hair-brained, rash and utterly foolish thing I ever did in my life. ●

CHAPTER THIRTY-ONE

I found Mark Kenny's section of the research labs easily enough. It was the area where the six burly men in U.S. Army uniforms were packing up boxes, removing filing cabinets, tossing computers into a cart as if they were sacks of potatoes. They were all disassembling counters, disconnecting gas lines and even getting ready to take down the light fixtures. Mark Kenny's section of the lab, as well as that of his assistants apparently, was being completely removed.

The whole thing struck me as just a bit off. Yes, the half-dozen rough and readies doing the demolition work looked quite efficient and strong enough to work for quite some time without a break. But, from the amount of work already done, it looked as if they'd been at it for half the day. Even if I was wrong by fifty percent, by seventy-five even, that would still mean they'd started their work before Kenny had killed himself.

For those out there that aren't following my drift, that last fact was highly suspicious.

I had set myself to watching the proceedings from the stairwell I had taken downstairs. It had a large enough window through which I could spy on the proceedings, and was close enough to the room in question that I could catch the odd phrase or two. I wasn't in position more than two minutes when one of the boys in green complained about how long they'd been working. Bingo, I thought, he'd just confirmed for me that they'd been ordered to removed Kenny's entire lab something like four hours before he'd shot himself.

Wiffalon'd been right. Something was dirty in the bowels of Haberton. But, what? My mind started racing. I still thought my idea of Kenny getting rid of Wendel so he could move in on Veronica was solid. If so, what did this cover-up mean? It was known that the university had a massive R&D complex, and that they dealt with the military. None of this was any kind of secret. So, I wondered, just what was it that was being concealed from the public this time, and exactly how high up did this need for concealment go?

Just as I wondered that last bit, Fate decided to cut me a break. As I continued to spy on the proceedings as carefully as I could, Carmine Esposito came into view, shouting orders in all directions. Then, with kind of a chuckle in his voice, he informed everyone that he had just finished being briefed by the local law on Kenny's suicide, and that the sheriff and the coroner were going to be coming in first thing in the morning to check out the lab. When Esposito spoke of Jeeter's request that the lab be sealed until his arrival, his voice took the same humorous tone it did when he had mentioned Kenny's suicide.

"We'll have this room emptied in another hour, guaranteed, major," one of the troopers said to Esposito. My ears perked up at the word "major." I had been snapping pictures through the window at every safe instance. I took an unsafe chance to catch one of supposed civilian Esposito returning his sergeant's salute.

"Good work," answered the major. "There's a crew on its way with those bits and pieces we don't have here in stock. I trust we'll have a new laboratory for the sheriff to pour over stupidly in wonder tomorrow?"

"By midnight, sir," the sergeant replied. "Down to the stained coffee pot and all of Kenny's dorky little cartoons."

Esposito took his leave then, returning the soldiers to their many and varied tasks. He called out that he would be in complex Alpha if anyone needed him, then continued down the hallway without a backward look. Leaving me, of course, with quite a quandary.

There was, of course, nothing I could do to halt the removal of the lab. I had documentation that it was being done--had caught Esposito and his sergeant on my trusty old tape recorder, even had my pictures to back that up. Letting the soldiers know I knew what they were doing would probably result in my own "suicide," I figured, so interfering with them was simply out of the question.

I could call Jeeter on my cell, but whoever had that bugged would know I made the call. Considering what I'd just witnessed, I had a pretty good idea who'd done the bugging. And the drugging. But, I asked myself, even if I made it to another phone and called the sheriff, what would I tell him? What could he do? My only "proof" that Kenny maybe didn't kill himself was a bit of "wink and a nod" between Esposito and the sergeant. Nothing Jeeter could use to get a warrant.

Besides, I asked myself, since when did I become a policeman? I wasn't hiding there behind a door to solve a crime. I was there to get a story. And, the only thing close to a story that I could sell anyone on printing was walking away from me. The segment of my guts where my instincts are held was screaming at me that whatever I was looking for I was going to find it in complex Alpha.

Summoning up all my nerve, I stepped out of the stairwell and turned in the direction in which Esposito had disappeared. I walked past the lab area without paying it the slightest mind, as if soldiers dismantling equipment in the basement of a university building was as common a sight as carnations at the Rose Bowl Parade. I didn't look at them, and they didn't look at me.

Once past the door, I hurried along to try and catch up with Esposito. I didn't want to come up alongside him, of course, but if I lost sight of which way he went I figured that was it for my story. In just a few seconds I caught sight of him and slowed my pace considerably. As he turned a corner, I hurried up again, trying desperately to keep him in sight without letting him know he was being followed, and to ignore the part of my brain that was screaming at me about what a horse's ass I was being.

I knew I was being crazy, that the risk seemed totally out of proportion with whatever reward I might garner. For some reason, it just didn't seem to matter. Wearing Esposito's coat had gotten me dirty looks from every other person in town. I knew it was insane, but I was simply sick and tired of taking the heat for the guy. On top of that, however, was the less rational but more personal fact that he'd played me for a sap. If he was behind Kenny's death, if these plant-things really were built for the military, then he had to know about them... and he had to have known about them all along. I just couldn't let him get away with all of it.

After another pair of turns, Esposito came to a doorway with the word "Alpha" stenciled on it in white paint. Outside of its keypad lock, it seemed as ordinary as any basement door anywhere. That lock was going to be trouble, though, unless...

Grabbing my camera, I used its lens control to bring distant images as close as possible. Then, I focused on the keypad and prayed Esposito was right-handed. He was. I kept myself from blinking, watched as closely as I could, and got five out of six numbers--5 ... 3 ... 2 ... 8 ... 8 ...

And that was it. The last number was another "8" or a "9," but I wasn't certain which. As Esposito disappeared inside, I weighed my options. I could just as easily get out while the getting was good and find Jeeter, tell him everything I knew, and then let him and the state police handle things. If there was anything to handle. Again, we were talking potentially very dangerous people who covered their tracks very carefully.

"For all you know, Carl," I muttered to myself there in the hallway, "he could be going in there to oversee the clearing out of everything in there as well. By midnight he could be clean as a whistle, completely untouchable, and where will your story be then?"

It was true. I'd just be crazy old Kolchak, again. Yelling about monsters, making everyone shrug and groan. I could hear Updyke snickering at me, could see Morgan Slate shaking his head sadly, could see Tony looking angrily disappointed. I was so sick of it, so painfully, finally, goddamned sick of it all that before I knew it, I had walked forward and stabbed the five numbers I was certain of into the key pad. Hesitating, I stared at the "8" and the "9," trying to decide between them. Would an alarm go off if I was wrong? Or because the same number had been repeated so quickly?

"Nine."

I heard the number in the back of my brain, and before my conscious mind knew what I was doing, I'd punched in that key. My heart froze solid, my blood stopped flowing. Unblinking, I stared at the door, waiting to see what would happen next. And, after the unbearably long wait of one point five seconds, the lock clicked open electronically.

I was in.

All I needed to do was find the nerve to pull the door open and enter. ●

CHAPTER THIRTY-TWO

Acting on impulse once more, before I could think my way into retreat, I grabbed the door handle and pulled. When I saw there was no one in sight on the other side, I slipped through the doorway into complex Alpha, then pulled the door shut behind me. As the lock clicked shut, I ducked into the shadows behind a large stack of crates and did the worst thing I could have done--I started to think about my situation logically.

Suddenly it dawned on me, where exactly was I going to go within ol' complex Alpha? What was I going to do--what was I looking for? Worse, how was I going to get back out? Did the door take the same code going out? A different one? Was I going to get myself shot?

Over the last few days I'd been allowing events to drive me. I hadn't thought anything out, merely been shunted along a series of rapids I could barely navigate. In fact, I thought, sitting in the darkness, suddenly terrified, suddenly alone, that's the way I'd been operating for years.

"Ever since that damn vampire," I muttered quietly. "Ever since Vegas."

It was true. Oh, I'd used my brains once something got started, but as I looked back, I began to realize I'd been herded along by events for years--years. Was that the way the weird and the supernatural worked? Once you were involved, once you no longer suspected they existed, once you actually knew--did everything under the sun somehow become attracted to you, or you to them?

It hadn't even been five years. Not even five stinking little years. And yet so much had happened to me, so much of this crap had followed me no matter where I had gone. And I had gone far– covered the country– in that time. Indeed, it seemed as if Tony and I had been moved about by Fate in every direction... ever since Vegas.

And then, just as my fear almost got complete hold of me, I wondered at that single word--Vegas. What was making me think about it so, about Janos Skorzeny in particular? Sure, I've thought about the past before, but it had never crawled down and curled around my spine like this, brought alive my old terrors, left me shaking ...

"What the hell is wrong with me," I wondered aloud. The longer I sat there in the shadows, second by second I felt myself falling into a deeper and deeper panic. At which point my uncle Gustav's voice came into my head. It was an old joke he loved to tell:

"A man goes to the doctor. He holds his arm out to the doctor and moves it up and down, and he says, 'Doctor, it hurts when I do that.' And the doctor says to him, 'Don't do that.'"

Without hesitation, I stood up. If sitting in shadows had started me panicking, then why was I doing it? Then, as I stood up, I turned around, looking further into the darkness, looking at the shelves I'd had my back up against. My eyes having adjusted to the darkness somewhat, I was able to make out shapes on the shelves. One in particular drew my attention—a sealed canister which had been directly behind my head as I'd been crouching. Why it attracted me, I couldn't tell you. Why I did what I did next, I could tell you even less about.

Stung by curiosity, I reached for the metal container. It was a small thing, a cylinder no more that ten inches high and five in diameter. Picking it up, I found it to be heavier than I had anticipated. Turning it over, I found a label. Moving it toward the light, I read what little it had to tell me, and felt true horror in every cell of my body.

JANOS SKORZENY; Remains

It couldn't be, I thought, I swore--I prayed. I'd seen him die. Watched him burn. It couldn't be be! It couldn't be!

And then I returned the canister to its place on the shelf and backed away from it. As I put distance between myself and the container, the rational side of my mind washed over my panic. Yes, I had driven a stake through Skorzeny's heart, but I hadn't seen him burn. I'd only seen the house I'd left him in burn. Could someone have recovered his ashes after the fire? But why? Why were they here in a college basement?

As I backed away from the spot where I had first hidden myself,

I felt my panic decreasing. Suddenly, no matter how the canister had gotten on that shelf, I knew it's label was correct. The thing did hold Skorzeny's remains. It had to. I had felt him, his monstrous, snarling presence, and it had frozen my mind, dragged me back to the horrible handful of days when my life had turned from merely being a losing streak into a nightmare I wouldn't wish on most politicians.

Putting some distance between myself and the unexplainable canister, I started to check out some of the other things tucked away there in the darkness. There was no order to any of it, no discernable pattern—things were just stuck on shelves wherever they might fit. Much that I stopped to examine I could not make heads or tails of. There were crates claiming to contain all manner of artifacts, with names I'd never before encountered--Skunk Ape, Moa, Pleiosaur, Sea Ape, Athol, Bunyip, Orange Eyes--a hundred more. I also found plenty of crates and canisters labeled UFO with dates and locations trailing after them.

I came across thick files, some crammed with photographs. They mentioned ghost stories and hauntings, cases of possession and incidents of witches, demons, whathaveyou. Some of them I'd heard of, most I hadn't. Some I had been there for. Coming across one I remembered in particular, a file marked MADELAINE/TREVI, I took the moment to open it. The first thing I came to was a photograph of a beautiful woman, one I recognized. She was blonde and curvaceous, long locks spilling down over her shoulders, a wide, thin-lipped smile, one accented by a perfect nose and bright, shining eyes that promised sweetness and magic.

Her name was Madelaine, and there'd been magic, all right, but not a lot of sweetness. She'd been a witch, and she'd killed people as easily as most of us crack an egg. I remembered her perfectly, and if I'd doubted that she was the broomrider I'd met, such notions would have been dispelled by the next photo in the file. It was a picture of me, diving out of the way of a car trying to run me down. A car with no driver.

I replaced the file as a cold sweat broke out on my forehead. Drops of it oozed down the back of my neck as well. What the hell had I stumbled into, and more importantly, who were these people? How had they gathered so much occult information? So many artifacts? And more over, so many that related to myself?

I started to wonder if the government might be involved in some way. The close proximity of Gore to Washington D.C., soldiers dismantling Kenny's lab, the Pentagon connection, the university building weapons of war out of monsters ...

And then it hit me. Suddenly I began to wonder if the conspiracy theory boys were as crazy as most of us think they are. I started taking pictures then, stealing photos from some of the files. Getting my recorder going, I started a running commentary on everything I saw. As I came to another section of canisters like the one which had been labeled with Skorzeny's name, I began to recite whatever they had marked on them. There were dozens of them tucked here and there, but their names meant nothing to me. Not until I found one—Bernhardt Stieglitz—and then everything fit into place.

Stieglitz had been a werewolf I'd encountered several years earlier. The werewolf I'd dreamed about the other night when too much booze and a little bit of government drugging had sent me over the edge. That in mind, I began a serious study for the other memory that had haunted my dreams that night. I found it, too.

This bit of evidence I found was larger than the others, a massive steel box big enough to hold the largest linebacker you've ever seen. It had enormous, tight-sealing snap-locks on it, three in total, all of which called out to me. Even though I hadn't found a label for the thing, some part of me knew what was in it. One after another, I threw open the latches. As soon as they were undone, I put both hands to work, pushing up the heavy lid. A smell of Spanish moss and anger leaked out as I did, and without having to look, I knew what I would see. But, while churchmen can go on faith, a reporter needs facts, and so I pushed with all my strength and flung the lid the entire way open.

I had to take a breath after I did so, had to back up to take it from the cleaner air in the hall, that not tainted by the reek coming out of the container I'd just opened. Then, once I was braced I moved forward and looked inside. I found just what I thought I would.

It was Peremalfait, a swamp monster I'd encountered in the sewers of Chicago, or I should say, it's dried, desiccated remains. I shuddered violently, nearly screamed. I don't care what that sounds like to anyone, either. You escape death, you get chased across the face of a major city by something from Hell, something no one will believe is really there—then when you know no one in the whole goddamned world is going to help you, you summon up enough guts from somewhere to stand up and kill the thing... and then you open its coffin after thinking it was out of your life for good, and we'll see who's made out of what. The fact I didn't just scream and start running blindly for the exit told me more about myself than I would have given myself credit for.

    I shut the lid faster than I'd opened it, snapped all the locks back into place and stumbled away from the shelves. Again my mind reeled--what was this place? How could they have gathered all the things they had? Why did so much of it concern me? And then, as I backed along the opposite wall, my hand came across something that made me stop and look. It was a box filled with plastic spheres. Taking one from the container, as I held it in the meager light coming from the main hallway, I saw what looked like a massive seed inside the plastic container. Without thinking, I took it out of the sphere to look it over. As I did, I happened to glance down and read the label on the box.

    LOUO-GAROU/PEREMALFAIT

    This was it, I realized. One of these was what Kenny had created, or helped create--what he had used to murder Wendel Halford. Part werewolf, part swamp creature--a hybrid. It had sounded fantastic, even to me, earlier, but there under the university, I'd seen the lab where it had been built, and there in the hallway I'd found all the noxious, raw materials used in the assembly.

    While I simply stood there, before I could think what to do, I heard a noise from the main hallway. Throwing myself against the wall as far into the darkness as I could, I shoved the seed into my overcoat pocket as the door I'd followed Esposito through opened once more. It was the soldiers I'd left back at the lab. They were moving crates inside complex Alpha. Thinking that they would be turning on the rest of the lights any second, I took off, moving as far down the darkened corridor I was in as fast as I could without making any noise.

    Coming to another door, I hesitated, looking for a keypad. It had none. Frozen, realizing I had no idea what might be waiting on the other side, I began to hear boot steps in the hall behind me. The soldiers were moving into the darkened corridor. The back of my mind screamed at me that it didn't matter what was on the other side, trouble was coming up behind me right then and there. Knowing I had only seconds, I muttered:

    "Ahhhh, in for a penny ..."

    And then pushed the door open and slid through to the other

side just as the hallway behind me flooded with light. There was no one waiting for me on the other side, a fact for which I mumbled a quick prayer of thanks. There was something waiting for me, however, something glowing and sinister which drew my attention even as it rekindled my dread.

In the center of the room stood a clear tank filled with water. Cylindrical, with a curved top, it stood on a set of metal legs, the water within it bubbling gently. But, it wasn't the slowly rising strings of bubbles which held my gaze, but that which floated within their path. That was an oval-shaped object recognizable around the world—a human brain. Of course, my mind wondered whose brain it might be. Spotting one of the standard labels I'd seen up and down the hallway, my eyes stole a glance, and in that instant my world was turned upside down. As my eyes went wide, and the air within my lungs froze in place, I simply stared at the two words scrawled on the label:

HITLER'S BRAIN

And then, doors opened behind and in front of me, and I knew I was doomed. ●

CHAPTER THIRTY-THREE

I was still staring at the tank when the laughter started cascading in all around me. As I slowly looked up, I found soldiers coming in through the doors, automatic weapons to the ready. They were not the ones having the party, however. Mixed in with them were a large number of lab coat types. They were the ones making all the merriment. And behind all of them was Carmine Esposito. He merely smirked. Irritated by his smug look, I snapped:

"What's so funny?"

"Oh, come now, Carl... Hitler's brain? My god, man–where's your sense of humor?"

And then I realized where I had seen the cylinder in the center of the room before. It had been a prop in an old B movie, "They Saved Hitler's Brain." As I stared at the stupid thing, Esposito offered:

"They sell them in the backs of various horror oriented magazines. When we saw our little baby here for sale, what can I say, we simply couldn't resist."

"Well, all right then. You've had your little joke on me." Straightening myself up, I put on my best innocent face and said, "but I really do have to be going. So, if one of you gentlemen would just point me to the door..." No one seemed to find that line as funny as my moment of belief. Looking around at all the grim faces, and the gun muzzles, I asked:

"Oh well, worth a shot. So, should I be raising my hands, or do you just shoot intruders and feed them to the zombies?"

Several of the science-types nodded, whispering to each other. Esposito told the soldiers they could lower their weapons, actually dismissed all but one of them. Turning back to me, he asked:

"I'm assuming you're not going to make a great fuss, Carl. At least not until you hear my proposal?"

"You have an offer for me?" This, I could not wait to hear.

"Oh, yes; one you've earned. Please do understand, Carl, if we hadn't wanted you to come here, you would never have made it inside complex Alpha. Your progress was monitored from the time you entered Alpha Approach Hall B. Our cameras are state of the art; don't beat yourself up for not being able to spot them."

Somehow, the back of my mind whispered, when the time comes for it, we probably wouldn't have to worry about me beating myself up.

"You came across some old friends out there in the hallway, didn't you?"

Something in Esposito's tone made me snap. What I had seen in the hallway were not "old friends." It was a collection of horrors, of things from beyond the comprehension of most people, damned things that had no right to exist. After the past few years, I'd had enough. After the past few days, I'd had more than enough. Wheeling around, guards or no guards, I stalked up to Esposito and snapped;

"Might we can all the pleasantries? Cut past the nonsense? If you have some sort of offer for me, let's hear it. What gives around here? Who are you people--really? What goes on in this place? Are you government? Are you some kind of James Bond villains? What's with the monster gallery out there? And for that matter, how in hell did you even get half that stuff? I mean, I was there. I saw Janos Skorzeny die—saw him burn up. And, and..." As I stopped to catch my breath, Esposito said:

"Come, Carl—please; have a seat. Let me try and answer all your questions. Would you care for something to drink?"

I asked for a Scotch. One of the younger-looking lab boys was sent off after it. The others were reminded they had jobs to do. As they filtered out of the room, the one remaining soldier took a position at Esposito's side on the other side of a work table from the seat I'd been offered.

"Let's start at the beginning," said Esposito. "And that would be 1945, deep inside Germany."

I took a deep pull on my Scotch. Any story that starts with Nazis usually calls for a stiff bracer.

"I'll keep this brief," my host continued. "We all know that when the Americans and the Russians rolled into Germany, they gathered up all the scientists they could and packed them off to home to work on the space race. But, people tend to forget that Hitler had researchers working in occult areas as well. The United States was fortunate enough to come across the main Nazi occult research facility and thus netted the bulk of the Third Reich's supernatural investigators."

"No wonder you couldn't resist the Hitler's Brain prop."

"Exactly," said Esposito with a twinkle in his eye. "Now you're getting it. We actually have a plaque for it that says 'our founder.' You should be flattered. We threw the label on just to get a laugh out of you."

I toasted the floating plastic brain with my drink. Esposito smiled at the gesture, and continued.

"Their first big project was the Roswell aliens. Did you know there was no spaceship? No--they were creatures who actually flew through the currents of space. Remarkable find--taught them a lot about adaptive physiology. Anyway, the Germans and those Americans assigned to the project worked in the desert for a number of decades. You may remember some of the work they did filtering out to the media, reports of the C.I.A. using psychics, Wall Street consulting with witches, government tests into the paranormal--every few years there were a spate of stories.

"You see, the original idea was to eventually acknowledge Project Otherside's existence. But, as the research that was done here produced more and more results the government deemed Top Secret, that idea was changed. In the early eighties Area 51, the project's original home, was abandoned by Otherside. Too many of those watching the facility's entrances were coming close to getting an idea of what went on out there—outside of the airship tests, of course."

"The stuff they've been building by backward engineering other captured spaceships—since Roswell wasn't a ship crash?"

"You see," Esposito told his aide, "sharp mind, doesn't miss a fact. Despite all he's seen, and the rush of information that would overwhelm most men, Carl is right with us." He saluted me with his own drink, took a sip, then went back to the history lesson. I endeavored to continued to not be overwhelmed.

"For almost ten years Otherside was homeless, being shuffled from spot to spot, the government trying to find it the perfect home."

"And twenty years ago," I threw an educated guess into the ring, "they bought up Haberton and sent you here to oversee its transformation into Monster U."

"Pretty much, yes. Very good, Carl." I disliked the way he doled out his praise. It was a bit too condescending, as if he either thought no one could hear the tone in his voice, or he didn't care. I was beginning to get a better idea as to why everyone in town hated the sight of his coat.

"Yeah," I answered, "I'm a genius. So how do I come into all of this?"

"Why, I'm surprised, Carl. I thought certainly you'd know where you came into things. It was a few years back, when our news watch department came across noise coming out of Las Vegas that a local reporter was claiming a vampire was on the loose. We contacted the Nevada FBI central office, hoping for a lead, and found the local man there was actually feeding this reporter information. I flew out there myself immediately. After studying the Roswell aliens and our other finds for decades, the chance to play with actual vampire DNA, well, it had our boys spinning, let me tell you."

"Vampires have that effect, apparently."

"Yes..." Esposito said the word drily, as if he'd have made a different comment if he was free to. He was holding himself back, though, and I wasn't sure why. Lucky me, he cleared things up with his next few sentences.

"And that brings me to a funny story. We felt you could be quite useful to us, Carl. So, I pulled some strings, and got the officials in Vegas to back it. When their man went inside the house Skorzeny had rented, he pulled the vampire's corpse out the back way, then torched the house. After that, well, I'm afraid it was my idea that the local politicians there send you packing. Now, in my own defense I'll add that they were just itching to find an excuse to go back on their word to you, I just gave them the impetus."

I stared at Esposito as if his eyes had just popped out of his head and rolled down into his lap. Everything I had endured since Vegas, the ridicule, the firings, the abuse from my so-called colleagues and the industry, the drying up of sources as it got around that I was sadly insane--all of it was the fault of the man sitting across the table from me. The guy who thought the last few miserable years of my life was nothing more than a "funny story."

I wanted to strangle him. I was conscious of the armed guard standing at his side, the man staring directly at me, waiting for me to do anything that would allow him to justify his pay, but I almost leaped at Esposito anyway. I could barely control the impulse. Swallowing my rage, though, I asked:

"If I'm not being too intrusive, would you mind telling me why you thought that was a good idea? I mean, what the hell difference did it make to you? What did you and your goddamned Project Otherside get out of ruining my life?"

"Now Carl, you've got to see the big picture. With your ability to transcend conventional reality, to look at the facts and see the truth, no matter how insane that truth might seem, you were just what we needed. Discredited, no one would pay any mind to what you said. But, whenever we needed you, we could simply send some interesting information your way, or your editor's, or publisher's way, and get you out there digging for us once more."

"So, you're why none of my stories ever got printed--no matter how many facts or how much evidence I had? Why all that evidence would 'mysteriously' disappear? Why none of my photos ever came out? What... did you have your goddamned men in black shooting me full of x-rays every time I got something in focus?"

"Nothing so unsophisticated," answered Esposito with a chuckle. "You wouldn't have been any good to us with cancer."

"But..." I started to ask a series of questions, but surprisingly, they answered themselves. I'd wondered about a number of things over the years--like how it was that Vincenzo and I both kept ending up in the same cities, how we would get fired at the same time, why all the loony stories kept coming my way.

Now I knew; it had all been planned. It had all been arranged. I'd felt cursed half the time, wondering what kind of insane, savage god could keep throwing so much nutball shit in my way. And now I knew. That god was the government, and all I'd done to incur its wrath was be a free thinker. Oh well, I told myself, it wasn't like I was the first guy this had ever happened to. Just ask Socrates. Or Oscar Wilde.

"So, you turn me into a social outcast, make me doubt my own sanity, cost me love and fame and fortune, throw me in the path of horrors from beyond for years—for years—and now, now you have an offer for me. Oh, my stars and garters this ought to be good. I mean, taking a look at what you've done for me so far, I can't wait to see what this offer could be. Might there be a dental plan connected. But wait, don't tell me yet ..."

Hoisting my drink, I drained every last drop from my glass. It was good Scotch, and it went down smooth and easy. Smacking my lips, enjoying the aroma of it as the fumes curled across my tongue, I said:

"All right, thrill me, Carmine. I'm as drunk as I'm going to get, I guess, since I don't see a waiter with the rest of the bottle. Unless, of course, you've drugged me again."

"I guess we do have a few things to apologize for, Carl," offered Esposito as he signaled for someone to bring me a fresh drink. "I did start things as far as you were concerned, although I should point out that quite a number of the weird things you've come across, you did so all on your own."

"Lucky me."

"Yes, Carl--yes," he said with excitement. "That's exactly the point. You are lucky; you're clever, resourceful and intuitive. You're open to new experiences, you can cross-reference realities better than most of the people working here. You seem to have the perfect ability to remain skeptical up until the exact moment of proof has been gathered, and then you don't waste any time trying to make up your mind over whether something is real or not. You act--decisively. Do you know how rare an ability that is?"

"Well, I ..."

"Carl, Janos Skorzeny escaped a dozen times over the years simply because those who figured out exactly who and what he was failed to believe the proof right there before their eyes. You're not that kind of man."

"Okay," I said, "then what kind of man am I?"

"The kind," Esposito said, his body language and voice conveying as much sincerity as he could muster, "I'm hoping would be willing to think about a career change."

As my drink arrived, I saw that Esposito had apparently signaled for one for himself. As the identical pair of glasses were set on the table, he said:

"I was over fifty when I came here, Carl. I've put in twenty years. It's time for me to retire."

"Yeah," I said, grabbing up my glass. "And so...?"

"And so, Carl, I'm asking you ... would you consider becoming the head of Project Otherside?" ●

CHAPTER THIRTY-FOUR

I didn't remember picking up my second Scotch, but when my eyes finally blinked, I looked down and noticed that it was two-thirds empty. My mouth still feeling dry, however, I picked it up and finished it off with a conscious gulp. As I swallowed, I stared at Esposito, wondering if too many years underground had taken its toll on him. How could he claim to know me so well, and then think I would do such a thing?

Still, the incredibly practical side of my mind asked, what would be so wrong with it?

In an instant everything positive about such a move flashed through my mind. It compared Esposito's car to mine, his clothes to mine, reminded me that his cast-offs were luxuries to me. Carl Kolchak, president of a university. Me, in charge of one of the government's most highly prized secrets. Uncle Gustav's favorite nephew, a respected member of society. Finally.

No more flea-bag apartment. No more one stinking, lousy suit in the closet. No more chasing pointless stories or being harassed by pinheaded bureaucrats. No more barking dogs or doors being slammed in my face. No more Morgan Slate, Ron Updyke, or Tony Vincenzo. No one in charge of me, above me, watching me, giving me orders, except who? The president? It could be a nice change, just like eating in restaurants every night just might beat Raman noodles and Vienna sausages every night.

Every goddamned night.

"You look as if you're considering my little offer." Esposito's face was all smiles. I guess he could see how I felt about the advantages he was offering me. Seeing that look, however, instantly reminded me of the other end of those scales.

Not even thinking about the fact we were talking running an organization started by Nazis, something I'm certain Uncle Gustav wouldn't have approved, there were a few more concrete things to take into consideration. Like the fact these people were gathering horrors from beyond and crafting them into weapons. Just thinking of the bodies littering the local countryside made my blood run cold. Thinking about the fact Esposito had sentenced another man to death for causing them made it run colder. Kenny was a murderer, and for a scientist, not a very bright one, but I didn't care how convenient his "suicide" was for everyone, it was still a cover-up, and it still fried my Polish ass.

"Oh, dear," came Esposito's voice. "Now you're not finding my offer so interesting, are you?" I give the man credit, he could read people. Curious, I asked him:

"You're still a fit looking guy, Carmine. Why are you giving all this up? One look at Congress, and you know this government doesn't believe in mandatory retirement. And you seem to enjoy your work. So, why are you even leaving?"

"I wasn't going to mention this yet, had hoped to get you to say 'yes' without the extra inducement, but..." it was obvious whatever it was it was something important. For the moment, Esposito's glibness vanished, as if whatever nerve I'd struck took real consideration before talking about it. Finally, I could see in his eyes he'd made a decision. Taking a deep breath, he confirmed my suspicions as he told me:

"Twenty years is a long time to do the same thing. Couple that with the fact that I'd still be in the background as a consultant, and it's not as clean a break as it sounds. But frankly, now that I've accepted part of the rewards package we have here, I'm simply dying to get out in the world and put it to good use."

I stared, waiting for him to drop the other shoe. Seeing that he had my attention, he let it fall. The thud it made was resounding.

"I'm over eighty years old, Carl. I know I don't look it. That's because, thanks to our researchers, we've discovered, for lack of a better name, the fountain of youth. You've lead us to vampires, mummies, books of dark wisdom, plus all manner of other bits and pieces of arcania which have allowed us to crack the whip in death's face. We've isolated a serum that, with yearly booster shots, gives one youth and strength and vitality." Catching the obvious look in my eye, he said:

"And no, no virgins have to be slaughtered, no blood has to be drunk. That was the dark ages. These things are much simpler now, aren't they, my dear?"

I could hear the footsteps behind me, knew who it was from their seductive rhythm on the floor, but I turned anyway. It didn't matter that I knew who it was. I had to look. I needed feedback from more than a single sense before I started cursing Fate for once again signing me up to play King of the Idiots.

"It's true, Carl," she said. I watched the words come out of her perfect lips and my heart shattered. "How old do you think I am?" When I said nothing, she told me:

"I'm sixty-two, Carl. Do I look it? Does my skin feel like that of a sixty-two year old woman? We're you thinking of grandma when you were spanking me?"

I muttered "no" to each question, my insides curling, knotting, my lungs tightening, veins throbbing. Suddenly the room was too hot for me. I asked for a glass of water, which Esposito summoned immediately. I also asked if I might take off my overcoat. Suddenly my vampire host's old coat, picked out for me by his ageless whore, seemed to heavy to keep wearing.

"You're an intelligent man, Carl," LuAnn said, "so I know you're up to speed. Yes, I was assigned to get close to you. Yes, I drugged you, bugged your room, read through your stories, that was my job. But no one said I had to enjoy myself. That was my idea."

I threw the overcoat on a nearby console, one close to Esposito. It was his coat, after all. Like his job, I didn't want it. As I took the glass of water the guard brought back, I drank deeply. What did it matter if it was drugged, poisoned, luke-warm? It was their game, and I'd hit every ball to exactly the section of the park where they'd wanted it. Not done with me, though, LuAnn came closer. Getting on her knees before me, she looked into my eyes and told me:

"Part of my job was to evaluate you, to see if you were the right man to oversee things here. You've got to remember, you're not being asked to build weapons, or kill children--nothing like that. You're being asked to lead people into every corner of the world, searching for the unknown, shining lights into all the dark places until the truth is known. Every legend, every myth, every lost treasure, you'll be in charge of uncovering them all, and bringing the benefits to mankind."

"Because they have other people to build the weapons, right," I asked. "And to kill the children."

LuAnn's face changed as if she'd been slapped. It didn't go cold and dark. I could see it. She honestly cared for me. She really believed in me, wanted me to stay there, couldn't understand how I could turn it all down. I didn't despise her or anything else melodramatic. Hell, a large part of me couldn't understand how I could turn it all down, either. Especially her.

"I don't think he's going to agree," came Esposito's voice. "Are you, Carl?"

I was just about to depress everyone with my answer when the lights began to flash red and yellow, and a barking series of alarms filled the air. ●

CHAPTER THIRTY-FIVE

"Marines!" A voice shouted the single word through a loudspeaker, then followed up with, "They—they're... they're everywhere, sir. Across the campus. Hundreds--probably a full battalion of light infantry."

"Goddamnit!"

Esposito came up out of his chair as if it were on fire. Turning to the console behind him, he grabbed up a microphone and started barking orders. Soldiers and scientists came streaming through the room, some moving with purpose, others clearly in a panic. Not having the slightest idea what to do, I nobly remained at my post, trying to figure out why U.S. military men would be attacking a U.S. installation. As I did, LuAnn stood up, grabbing me by the wrist.

"Com'on," she said, her eyes wide with panic, "we've got to get out of here."

"Why?" I asked, not resisting so much as just trying to understand. "What's going on?"

"Wake up, Carl," she snapped back at me with dark impatience. "Do you think only Latin Americans have coups?"

"Damn sons of bitches," Esposito snarled. "Think they're playing with amateurs, do they?"

"What're you going to do?"

"They want a war, Carl," answered Esposito, "we'll give it to them. Don't think the Louo-Garou/Peremalfait is the only thing we have to throw at them. From the aliens, from the hard tech UFOs we've recovered, from the books of the elder gods... we've got an arsenal of monsters and hellfire down here undreamed of since St. John the Divine wrote the Book of Revelations!"

Gunfire broke out in the halls to both sides of us. I looked at my water glass, wishing I'd asked for another Scotch instead. As I tried to pick a path of action, several explosions rocked the room. Then, after more gunfire, a marine pushed his way through the door from which Esposito had first entered. Seeing mostly civilians, he hesitated. Although I'm glad he didn't start shooting at everyone in the room, it was a mistake for him not to do so.

Turning from him with a speed I could scarcely follow, LuAnn spun around and drove her hands directly into the man's chest. Before he could react, before he could even utter a syllable of pain or shock or condemnation, her hands shattered his ribs, grabbed his lungs, and ripped them from his body.

Throwing the organs on the floor, she wiped her hands on his uniform before he could react, then plucked his weapon from his hands as he toppled over backward. Moving forward, she emptied his automatic rifle into whomever had been coming down the hall behind him, then with that same blurring speed returned to his body in search of more ammunition.

At his console, Esposito continued to give orders. I knew he had to be at least as fast and strong as LuAnn. I knew I didn't stand the slightest chance against him. But, I also knew that if there was anyone in the entire place he was not going to let escape alive, it was me. That thought foremost in my mind, I stood up, ready to try and jump him. Remembering my water glass, I grabbed it up, hoping that if I couldn't stop Esposito with it, I might be able to allow him to share a bit of the pain he'd doled out to me over the years.

And then, it happened.

Next to Esposito on the console, my overcoat began to twitch. As I stared at it, second after second, with gunfire ringing in the corridors all around me, I watched as it flopped and bucked more and more violently, and then finally began to unravel. My mind racing, I tried to imagine what could be happening, and then it dawned on me. The seed, the damned werewolf-swamp monster seed. I had stuck one in my pocket.

But, even as I watched the coat shudder once more, I couldn't find a reason for it to be happening. All I had done was remove the thing from its package. There was no soil in my pocket to activate it. Or blood ...

Blood!

The gloves, Wiffalon's bloody gloves that I'd shoved in my pocket, the seed was feeding on the blood, on the wool fibers of the jacket. But, even if it were growing, I wondered, how long would it take to grow to its killer stage?

How long?

Time froze within my head as I stared at the coat. No one else seemed aware of it. Not Esposito barking his orders. Not LuAnn, spraying the hallway with bullets. Not the rest of the soldiers under their command, blockading the other entrances. The explosions in the complexes beyond, the hundreds of gunshots, the agonizing screams of the dying, the never-ending sirens—all of it pounded together, creating a maddening cacophony that forced everyone to ignore everything but their most immediate task. Mine just happened to be watching an overcoat turn into a monster.

It started with green-gray tendrils, bursting through every seam, out of sleeves, through the collar. The rate of ingestion must have been exponential, for once the thing started to transform in earnest it was done in seconds. My coat was gone, and growing its way into the console was the thing from my nightmare.

"Holy Christ in Heaven!"

The confused cry of the soldier who first spotted the thing did not reach anyone else. There was far too much noise for anyone else to hear. Indeed, I'm only guessing what I thought I saw his lips say. But, he reacted true to his training and brought his weapon to bear on the creature and fired. Bullets tore through pulpy flesh harmlessly. I watched wounds appear, and then grow over in seconds. The soldier watched as well, stunned into immobility. The creature took advantage of that fact and sent its tendrils whipping in his direction.

Esposito, who may not have heard the man's exclamation, heard the gunfire that followed. Becoming aware of the growing creature, seeing it reaching for the trooper, he grabbed up a chair with the same amazing speed LuAnn had shown earlier, trying to stop the thing from reaching its prey. He was too late.

The chair tangled in the grasping, claw-hooked vines, but did not stop them from reaching the soldier, piercing his skin, drawing on his blood, his flesh, whatever it needed to grow larger, to defend itself, just as it's scientist parents had taught its recombined DNA to do. The man was torn apart in seconds, all of us in the room splattered with his blood.

Esposito should have known better. They had given their creations the instinct to attack whatever attacked them. The soldier went down first. Esposito was next. With a speed that rivaling that of its creator, the plant-thing didn't even bother to turn around. It simply grew a dozen new appendages in Esposito's direction--biting, fang-tipped branches which clamped onto his skin, chewed into his muscles, refusing to let go.

As he howled, tearing off limbs and hurling them away, only to be attacked by new growth, LuAnn somehow sensed his agony over the sea of noise. Turning, spotting his dilemma, she abandoned her post at the door, first slamming its locks into place, then racing to help Esposito. I backed away from the struggle, horrified as green and red fluids were splattered from all those in the small battle.

Not backing away far enough, I got splashed across the face by a wave of blood torn from LuAnn's mid-section. Snapping me back to reality, I realized the only thing I could do was to get the door LuAnn had locked open again. Deciding there was no time for subtlety I ran for it. I could tell from the way it was vibrating that someone or several someones were throwing themselves against it on the other side. Just as I reached it, they accomplished their task, knocking the drop bolts free and opening the door.

At the console, Esposito and LuAnn had pulled their efforts together and ripped the plant-creature in two, tearing its digging roots free from the console. Esposito slumped over, crashing back against the wall from the effort. LuAnn stumbled backward, grabbing for anything she could to steady herself.

As she did, my mind pieced together what was happening as agent Boll came storming through the doorway with several marines. She began to take aim at LuAnn, but the immortal government clerk had not only already caught herself, but had begun to bring her own weapon up. Logic knew what I had to do, but in the split-second given to me to decide what I was going to do, I relived every moment we had shared—not just the bedroom, but the laughter, the teasing, the falling in love which I knew, I damn well knew was shared by both of us.

I felt every bit of emotion in one raw instant that I had experienced since I'd been in town, realized that my actions either way could turn the tide--I could still be everything Esposito had offered, including immortal. I could have wealth and fame and power—have it forever—with the first woman I'd loved in years at my side-right now, and then down through the ages.

As everyone around me seemed to move in slow motion, I saw LuAnn's weapon coming up, saw Boll trying to bring her own to bear, and taking the glass I was still holding, I summoned up every over-home-plate moment of my little league days and sent it flying. It smashed against LuAnn's face and shattered into a hundred pieces. Digging into her skin, rupturing one of her eyes, knocking out several teeth. Two seconds too late.

I screamed in regret as a burst from LuAnn's automatic tore through Boll and sent her flying backwards. As I ran to her side, the marines concentrated their fire, a score of bullets knocking LuAnn backwards, slamming her into the console. I reached Boll at the same time Norman did. I was amazed she was still alive.

"We're going to get you out of here," I screamed, trying to be heard over the din.

"Forget it," she shouted back, blood bursting over her lips. "Done for. Can't even ..."

And then she was gone, eyes wide open, mouth agape, head hanging limp. I stared at her, tears filling my eyes for the awkward, weak-chinned horse of a woman who had just saved my life by throwing hers away. I might have knelt there until it was too late, but Norman grabbed my arm, jerking me to my feet as he screamed in my ear:

"Com'on--we've got to get out of here!"

As I was snapped erect, my eyes went to the battle at the console. Esposito was down, leaking rivers of blood from three gaping wounds—two in his chest, one in his head. LuAnn was still, torn in half by the marine gunfire. The plant-thing was finished as well, but not because of its vampire parents.

When ripped from the console, it had torn something inside that started it burning. It must have grown far into the machinery, for not only was the creature on fire, but the console as well. As Norman pulled me toward the door, he was shouting at the marines, telling them to pull back.

We made it as far as the hallway before the smell of electrical smoke reached us. In a handful of seconds, the explosions which had seemed far away before were suddenly all around us. After that, the ceiling began to fall, and darkness descended. ●

EPILOGUE:

"So, enjoy your stay in Gore?"
 I looked across the table in Larry's at Sheriff Jeeter as if he were a chimp flinging crap at me. Campbell, possessing all the subtlety of a Klansman, added:
"Oh, he's just sorry he lost his new coat."
They were just playing with me, the way friends do, trying to divert my attention, even willing to take my anger if that would help. Pulling down a lungful of air, I wheezed at the deputy:
"Turns out it was only a loaner."
Both of the lawmen smiled, not so much at the humor, but at the fact I could make the attempt at creating some. Norman nodded thoughtfully. Ididn't bother asking what he was thinking about.
I owed all of them my life. It turned out my FBI agents hadn't told me about all the listening devices LuAnn had hidden in my room. He had found one in my coat as well. He'd left it there without telling me, clipping one of his own right alongside it to see where I might be able to lead them.
Jeeter and Campbell, when they'd realized I'd gone missing, had informed my friends in the agency to the fact. It turned out several groups within the government were concerned with what had been going on at Haberton for a while. As things heated up after the murders started, Norman and Boll had contacted a major Timothy Snowden of Naval Intelligence, a fellow I'd met before when I'd met them and let him know their break might be coming. As Norman explained it, they'd had the marines on standby the whole time, waiting for something to happen. Something named Carl Kolchak.
I wasn't upset. It almost surprised me that I wasn't, but I simply didn't have it in me. Not in the aftermath of what had happened. Norman and I barely made it out of the complex. A lot more good men weren't so lucky. In fact, a lot of good people weren't nearly so

lucky as we were.

Haberton was completely destroyed. The fire started in Esposito's main control panel caused tremendous havoc, releasing God only knows what into their miles of underground tunnels. At present there is no telling what set off the apocalyptic explosions that opened the earth and swallowed the university. There will be an investigation, of course, and I'm quite certain there will be an extensive excavation. Jeeter is already planning to keep a careful eye on the area as soon as the bulldozers start showing up.

The college wasn't the only thing to topple. The devastation dropped thousands of acres into the ground, crossing the state line into West Virginia. Mountains were actually toppled. Mountains. The news crews that survived are all battling for their Pulitzers.

Of course I filed my stories as well. My Brooklyn turtle reported that Slate wants to give me a raise. I told him I would have asked for that in writing, but that I was fairly certain he couldn't write. That brought the blessed relief of a slammed cell phone lid, meaning I didn't have to listen to Vincenzo's voice again until I reached California.

For a moment, I honestly considered walking home.

I didn't try to tell all that I knew about the story. Esposito was right. I had been thoroughly discredited, and it was going to take a long time to get myself back on track. But, I thought, at least no one would be pulling Tony's and my strings anymore. The shadow puppeteers were gone, torn apart or crushed or burned to death, and we were free men once more.

And as a free man, I told the story the way I saw it. I called the incidents which had brought me to Gore the Crime of the Century. But not because of the levels of blood and horror. I deemed it such because it wasn't a single killer that had been triumphed over, but a cabal of madmen, monsters using our own tax dollars to victimize the nation.

I reported that the reason government relief troops were on the scene so fast was that they were there arresting a rouge government agency—the one responsible for the murders across two states. I didn't mention monsters and men in black. Why bother? I couldn't get most people to believe as much as I did tell them. But there were plenty who did, who understood that when their own government started treating them like bags of airline peanuts rather than human beings that it was time to start making some noise about it. What the hell, I told myself, it was a start.

In the two days since all the shooting had stopped, and the fires had all been extinguished, I'd had a lot of time to think. I'd turned in some of the best stories I'd ever written, attended a closed-casket service for the bravest FBI agent I figured I would ever meet, and swapped enough lies with Larry, and the other members of our impromptu gentleman's club to last me for a while. Looking around at the sorry lot, I lifted my coffee mug, the contents of which were definitely Irish, and said:

"My brothers, one last time, to Linda Boll. A hell of a woman when the chips were down."

Everyone toasted her along with me. And, in that moment, I felt a tremendous weight lift from my shoulders. Maybe my life was never actually going to change. Maybe I was slated to be Fate's garbageman the rest of my life. Well, I thought, so what? It kept life interesting. And, with complex Alpha and all its Nazis bastards off my back, finally, maybe it might start dishing up a little fun once in a while, too.

Larry took our orders after that and headed for the kitchen. As he did, Norman commented that I seemed to be in better spirits. I agreed with him that I just might be. At that point, Jeeter cleared his throat. Acting somewhat apologetic, he said:

"I'm glad to hear that too, Carl." Not liking the tone in his voice, I asked him what was up. He told me.

"You remember back when we rushed off to the campus, and you left your rental car in my spot?"

"You told me to."

"I know, I know. But one of my boys, one of the younger ones, he didn't know anything about that ..."

"Wait a minute, Jeeter ..."

"Yeah, I wish I could do something about it, but you see..."

"Now hold on here," I shouted a bit too loudly. As heads began to turn, I added, "You can't mean ... you wouldn't ..."

"I hate to do it," he went on, pulling a familiar style rectangle of paper from his inside jacket pocket. "But yeah, he wrote you this summons ..."

"This is the thanks I get? For all the help I was around here? For saving the world?"

"Now really, the fines here aren't like they are in the big city ..."

I was on my feet by then, waving my hat and shouting something about the second amendment. I'm not certain why I chose that one, but I believe it sounded good nonetheless. Just as I put a foot up on my chair to further emphasize my outrage, Larry returned from the kitchen with several baskets of fried chicken wings and onion rings. As he came up to the table, he said in an exaggerated drawl:

"Showed him the ticket, did ya?"

The bunch of them started laughing, and after several seconds of indignation and hurt feelings, I joined them. My laughing at myself started them laughing harder, and that set me to howling and banging on the table. Grabbing up a tiny chicken drumstick, I threatened the others with, then burned my mouth when I bit into it.

And that started the laughter all over again. I can't explain it. Maybe we were all simply glad just to be in one piece. All I know is for myself, for once, I felt like I had friends, and it was good to be with them. It was good to laugh. It was good to be warm, to have hot food and stiff drinks with which to wash it down. It was good to be alive.

Or to put it simply—finally—it was just damn good to be free. ●

ABOUT THE AUTHOR

CJ Henderson has a long history as a writer that makes him keenly perfect for the job of bringing Carl Kolchak alive once more for his millions of fans. A long time mystery and horror writer, his first world-wide hit was his character Teddy London, a private detective who accidentally stumbles across what may or may not be a supernatural occurance. His further investigations into the bizarre and paranormal spawned some five further novels (soon to be seven), more than two score short stories, a comic series and more than one movie option. (The RPG game for the character comes out next year.)

So popular did London become in such a short space of time that Henderson was approached by both the Lin Carter and the HP Lovecraft estates to revitalize their supernatural detectives. These projects met with rousing success as well. Moonstone, publisher Joe Gentile, a long-time fan of Henderson's private detective work, first asked the author to adapt his hardboiled PI Jack Hagee for comics. When the company aquired the Kolchak license, Henderson was one of the authors asked to turn out graphic novels for the character. His entries in their highly successful Nightstalker series met with such acclaim it was decided that, due to his long connection with the Lovecraftian mythos, Henderson would be the first author in both print and comics to introduce the long-suffering reporter to the worlds of HPL. After fan reactions to those works were reviewed, it seemed no contest--Henderson would be the company's choice to produce the first new Kolchak novel in over a decade!

Over the thirty years of his professional career, CJ Henderson has written some fifty books and novels, plus hundreds of short stories and comics as well as literally thousands of non-fiction pieces. For those who would like more information on the author and his works, or who would simply like to tell him what they thought of this novel, he welcomes all at his website, www.cjhenderson.com. Besides the regular history and news, he also posts free short stories there for those who just want a little something extra. ●

LAI WAN: Tales of the DREAMWALKER

Collected Tales of Terror from
C.J. HENDERSON
John L. French, Bruce Gehweiler, Patrick Thomas, and John Sunseri

"Lai Wan is nicely developed, yet shrouded in mystery."
—Ain't It Cool News

ALSO AVAILABLE

DARK FURIES: Weird Tales of Beauties and Beasts with stories C.J. Henderson, James Chambers, Adam P. Knave, Patrick Thomas, William Jones and many more!

The Case-files of THOMAS MALONE
H.P. Lovecraft's "The Horror At Red Hook," followed by C.J. Henderson's smashing sequel, "The Power of Fear." With a stunning wraparound cover by Ben Fogletto!

MARIETTA PUBLISHING

available online at
CJHenderson.com

MOONSTONE™

Comic Books!
Graphic Novels!
Prose Anthologies!
Novels!

The Phantom
Kolchak the Night Stalker
Buckaroo Banzai
Doc Savage
Sherlock Holmes
The Spider
Wyatt Earp
The Cisco Kid
and etc.

moonstonebooks.com

AMAZING FANTASY BOOKS & COMICS

Super Subscription Service

Never miss an issue of your favorite mag ever again!

Since 1978, **Amazing Fantasy** has offered an efficient & easy way for readers to get their comics!

*Free shipping (USA only)

*Free copy of Diamond's Preview Mag every month!

*order ANY product you want in the Previews!

*10% off everything you buy!

Just tell us which (8 or more) titles you want on a regular basis, and every month, you'll receive your books in the mail from us! You can change your pull list whenever you want with just an email! You can subscribe to a single issue of a title, or multiple copies, or just a mini series, or TPB's, manga series, or etc! (we are able to use credit card or paypal)

it IS as easy as it sounds!

We have sent out many 1000's of packages, and have been at it since 1978-so we mostly know what we're doing!

just contact us at: CONTACT_US@AFBOOKS.com